GEEZER DYKE
AND OTHER STORIES
OF BAD BEHAVIOR

GEEZER DYKE

AND OTHER STORIES OF
BAD BEHAVIOR

BECKY THACKER

she
said
books

GEEZER DYKE AND OTHER STORIES OF BAD BEHAVIOR

Copyright © 2024 Becky Thacker

All rights reserved

ISBN: 978-1-59021-605-7

TABLE OF CONTENTS

LIBRARY HOOKER

"Jane, come on, it'll be nice to ride together every day again. Remember how we did when I first moved over here? We haven't had any close time in like, forever."

Jane, stopped in the process of pulling on her sweater, just looks at her, shaking her head from side to side as though following an evenly-matched tennis match.

"Maybe just for another week? See how it goes?"

"No, Polly." Her voice is level; only Polly would recognize how short the fuse on this particular dynamite is getting. "The only place I'll drive you is to a car dealership."

Polly presses her lips together and in silence, she turns to her bag again. Wallet, check. Water bottle. Paperback of the latest Patricia Cornwell, already foxed and faded from the other night's Sleepy Time Tea mishap. She hoists the bag to her shoulder and offers, from under her ragged red bangs, a wistful look to Jane. Jane's warm brown eyes are glacial as she stares back.

"See you tonight," whispers Polly. Jane nods. Polly steps out into the early autumn air and pulls the door closed behind her. The crisp "Snick!" of the latch reminds her, too late, that she has left her door key hanging on the hook beside the door. She sighs and sets out for the bus stop.

Jane stares at the door for a moment more. She should open the door and hand the key to Polly, she knows, but the clump of ice in her chest weighs her down, pulling her shoulders down as well. So much she has loved Polly all these years, never noticing how much of that love has been curdling and then beginning to set, like Quikrete. She despairs of ever being able to chip it away again. She's given up trying.

Polly had ridden the Metro one time since she had moved to this Midwest city, as a lark and an experiment. She and Jane had walked the four blocks to the inbound stop, talking about, as was their family term, "cabbages and kings". The walk had taken no time at all.

Now, Polly's bag weighs more than she had expected and her work shoes pinch. Hurrying is not her strong point, but just now it seems a fine idea. She doesn't need her boss angry at her as well. The effort pays off; the number 58 is just closing its doors but the driver takes pity on Polly's awkward scramble and waits for her.

"Made it!" she says happily to the driver, who gives her the briefest of smiles and then turns his attention to the drive. "Bob" says the badge clipped to his pocket, and the brown smear that brackets it was from his daughter's nosebleed as he was leaving for work this morning.

The bus picks up speed and Polly balances against the pole so she can hoik her bag up and search within for her wallet.

"It's a dollar and a half, isn't it? Oh, no, I see, I see. Two and a quarter…um, do you have change?" The driver points to the "Exact change only" sign on the fare box. "Um, why don't I put this in and you can keep the change, then?"

"Suit yourself," Bob says, "It's your money, not mine."

Polly sways back to an empty seat, does a touch-and-go landing like a dragonfly on a lily pad and then sways to the front again. "When we get downtown, can you just let me off at Bankhill and Ohio Street?"

"We don't pass Ohio and Bankhill; we turn at Canton. Route map's behind me. Please take a seat and study it."

Polly returns to her seat and studies the map. The nearest route 58 stop is six blocks from her office. She wants to ask Bob if he can help her organize the transfer; her five dollar bill is in the fare box and she only has a debit card. A look at his set, intent face in the mirror convinces her not to. Yes, she'll be late, and yes, her feet will be as angry at her as Jane is and her boss will be.

"Oh, well," she says aloud. Her seatmate, a younger woman wearing a single ear bud that runs, Polly assumes, to a phone in her jacket pocket, gives her a skeptical look. Polly interprets this as interest. "Oh, well, things will work out. They always do. Nearly always, anyway." The woman looks away quickly, so Polly brings out her book and turns to the dog-eared page.

POLLY ALWAYS IMAGINES HER WORK week as those old movies that show the passage of time by pages falling, or on a good week, flying off a calendar. By the time the seventh leaf has dropped from her mental 1940s day-at-a-time calendar, she's riding the Metro with confidence, and even enjoying the process.

She now can size up the passengers; who will sprawl over too much of the shared seat, who is cranky and who is simply bored. This day she selects a teenager with what might be a goiter or might be the largest Adam's apple she's ever seen. He turns out to be remarkably garrulous for a teenage male, but after a couple of miles he talks himself out and proves to be a good listener, too. By the time they cross Grand Ave. she is telling him how she came to join the ranks of Metro commuters.

"Pickle kept breaking down, and I kept getting her fixed. Pickle was my last car; she was green but kind of old, so she had lumps and dents all over her…" The rider in the seat behind Polly and the boy emits an audible sigh and rattles a newspaper.

The teenager looks back nervously, but Polly doesn't notice, "I managed to find a garage that kept her running, but a couple of weeks ago, the power steering gave out with absolutely no warning. She'd been pulling really hard to the left for a while; the garage guy kept trying to align her but the shims wouldn't hold or something. So, when her power steering quit she went wandering across the center line and I smacked right into an SUV. I got a sprained wrist, is all, and the other driver was fine, but Pickle had to be towed away to the junk yard…"

The passenger in the seat behind them emits another sigh; it sounds like, "Oh, please".

"… I got a check from the insurance company, not huge, but enough for a down payment and several more payments. Just haven't gotten around to car-shopping. My partner Jane was driving me everywhere so there was no hurry to shop for a new car, but she was kinda mad that I let things go for so long…." Polly gives a helpless little laugh.

"Here's my stop," says the boy. He hops to his feet and is out the door just as Polly prepares to conclude her story by explaining about the glories of a weekly "ride all you want" bus pass that she has just purchased.

"Thank God," mutters the passenger behind Polly.

What Polly would have gone on to say, had the boy remained a bit longer, was that now she quite prefers riding the Metro. She is figuring out the routes and experimenting with side trips for other errands. Most recently she has decided to try out a lunchtime commute to the downtown branch of the library.

She and Jane used to use that branch when Polly first moved there. "They have reference books and more extensive nonfiction sections," Jane had told her, "And of course it's a really neat old building. No stone lions, but anything else a library needs, it has."

Polly'd been impressed. Fresh new library card in hand, she'd stood between the Doric pillars at the top of the stone steps and marveled at the diversity of patrons who lingered on the steps and the sidewalk below.

"How cool is that?" she whispered to Jane, "In this town even the hookers hang out at the library!"

"You goofball, they don't actually go into the library, they just hang out here."

"Oh."

Jane laughed at her crestfallen expression. "Well, maybe some of them are literary hookers, how would I know?"

"Let's say they are. Nobody spends their entire lives at their work, right?"

"Right."

As time went by and the sheen of first love wore thinner, however, Polly and Jane began to keep company with the library branch on the route home from downtown where they both worked.

*

POLLY NOW STEPS DOWN FROM number 17 Metro to the stately central library building that sits surrounded by older down-at-heel businesses and street folk, like a dowager who's seen better days. The front steps haven't lost their luster, for her, and as she comes back down to the bus stop, her new books in a backpack, she pauses and looks at the street theater below. Hookers, homeless folks, students, and occasional business-attired patrons of various sexes meander, strut, saunter and pose. A man of indeterminate age drags a cooler behind him, holding it by a sock threaded through its handle.

"I fit right in," she tells herself, knowing how untrue that actually is, and stations herself at the stop to wait for number 17 to come around again.

That evening she tries to tell Jane about it. Jane is sitting at her computer, a Styrofoam clamshell of salad at her elbow. When did they stop having dinner together at the table? Polly isn't positive, but it seems like only a few months ago. That was the day she'd forgotten her offer to pick up something at the grocery for Jane, who'd stormed out of the house and not come back for hours.

"You never remember anything I ask you to do!" was the gist of that incident, Polly recalls, and it was true. But "I don't remember things for myself either," she'd said to the closing door. Once upon a time, she considered ruefully, Jane had seemed to like her forgetfulness. "My absent-minded professor," she'd call her fondly.

"Jane! Remember the library hookers? I saw three of them today!"

Jane looks up, a glimmer of interest in her eye. "Really? Where?"

"At the central library. I took the bus there at lunchtime. Nothing has changed at all there."

"You're getting this bus thing figured out, huh? Good for you."

Polly beams and sits down on the arm of Jane's easy chair, but Jane has turned back to her computer and absented herself from the conversation.

By the fourth week of library visits, Polly recognizes some of the library folk and their habits. She marvels at how intuitively they divine the purpose of the cars that pull up at the curb and idle. Sometimes a pair of prostitutes will lean in to the passenger window and exchange a few words with the driver before one or both hop in. Sometimes it's a teenage boy or young man who leans in and rides away, and sometimes it's a man of indeterminate age. In the latter case, small packages may change hands along with folded cash. Sometimes the car will sit unmolested, idling for a few minutes before a library patron hurries down the steps, CDs or books in hand and boards the car.

In inclement weather, the street folk retreat to various shelters and lees: inside corners, abutments, doorways, and of course the bus stop shelter where Polly sits and tries to be unobtrusive.

"Nobody seems to bother them as long as they aren't too close to the front doors," she tells Jane that first rainy evening. "If they crowd the entrances, there's a library guard who shoos them away. Last week there was some other kind of guard who chased them out of the bus shelter."

Jane has put down her Kindle to listen. "Isn't it kind of creepy to have them come into the shelter when you're waiting in there?"

"I have to say, the homeless guys smell bad, especially in the rain. The prostitutes, well, I feel sorry for them. I moved over today to let one of them sit down. You know those awful spiky shoes they wear, it's like the Inquisition dreamed those up to punish women."

"Makes you wonder why guys want women who dress like that. Why don't they get turned on by a woman who looks comfortable in her clothes?"

"Maybe it's like they think the women are saying, 'I can't wait to get out of these uncomfortable clothes with you, you handsome brute.'"

Jane smiles and returns to her book.

"WOULDN'T YOU KNOW," POLLY THINKS ruefully the following week, "It has to rain on my library day." There's no reason in the world she can't wait for a nicer day, but her Wednesday library lunchtimes are becoming something she looks forward to, a break in the middle of the work week. She pulls on a slicker and goes anyway.

"Shee-yut," mutters the pimp behind her shoulder in the library portico, and Polly nods in agreement. She's waiting for a lull in the downpour so she can make a dash for the bus shelter. She hangs back in the lee of the portico with the man and one of the prostitutes, who leans against a pillar.

More patrons come out, crowding among the throng already there. A middle-aged white woman pulling a wheeled shopping trolley pauses to organize her belongings, squeezing the prostitute closer to Polly.

All the muscles on that side of Polly's body tense. "I will not pull away, I will not pull away, she's a person just like me, I will not pull away...." Polly pulls away a few inches; she's now more tightly pressed between the cart woman and the prostitute, and another person presses against her back. She tries not to think about substances dried on the back of the woman in front of her, or maybe ground into the faux leopard jacket on the woman next to her.

The prostitute fishes into the recesses of her fringed denim shoulder bag; incongruously, it has sequined owls on it. Fishing around for... a crack pipe? Switchblade? Hand-rolled cigarettes? Did anyone even carry switchblades around anymore? Guns, that's what people carried. Cheaply made, deadly handguns. Polly's shoulders are pinned up against her ears now.

The hooker pulls out a vintage paperback and opens it to a dog-eared page halfway through. The cover is missing; Polly knows that bookstores call such books "strips," meaning the cover is stripped off to prevent the resale of a book removed from circulation.

Polly forgets all about bodily fluids and deadly weapons. She can't resist edging toward the woman, hoping to catch a glimpse of the book's content. The woman's shoulders tense; she looks up beneath her brows at Polly as though she might growl a warning.

Polly looks casually away and opens the first book on her own stack. She steps back next to the prostitute in a casual way as though to get farther from the rain that spatters in, eyes on the page below her. "Don't read over people's shoulders, it's really rude," she chides herself, even as her eyes slip to the side and jump to the opposite page in the woman's hands.

"They're called breasts, Mama. Everybody has them," she reads, not aloud. Ah. Stephen King.

"If they only knew she had the power," murmurs Polly, unable to help herself.

"Huh?" The woman looks up sharply.

"Nothing. Sorry," says Polly, cheeks aflame.

The woman glares for an instant, but Polly knows that Carrie's torments are of more import to the reader than an impertinent comment from a stranger. Polly's sure she gets plenty of those in her day-to-day.

After a pause, the woman mumbles something that could be "Shut up," or "Sho nuff," or even "Shown up," and then returns to her reading.

It's like watching somebody else eat something delicious, how one's mouth waters in sympathy. Polly immediately hungers to travel in the spaces Stephen King has constructed especially for her. But she returns to her Ursula LeGuin classic and comes close to missing her number 17 bus.

"Wait, wait!" she yells, slamming the book shut and scrambling down the steps to the stop. She hears a chuckle behind her as she goes and knows she's given the prostitute something to smile about today.

"SHE WAS THERE AGAIN TODAY," Polly announces to Jane without preliminary the next Wednesday evening.

"'Oh, how you wish she'd go away'?"

"No, my library hooker. The same one. You know how cold that wind was today. And the rain, on and off. Everyone was crowded in the bus shelter to get out of it. She was there. At least she had slacks on today, but they didn't look very warm. Her ankles were bare, and she had these little flimsy shoes."

"You're sure it's the same one?"

"Yeah, she's still got the magenta streak in her hair. Anyway, she was leaning against the wall, reading another paperback. It was a really old one, just like the copy of Carrie she had before."

"Did you get a look at the title?"

"Not at first. I thought, as my mom used to say, 'I'd give a cookie to know' what it was."

"Maybe Plato's Republic. Or Hitchhiker's Guide to the Galaxy. You didn't ask her, huh?"

"I was afraid to. It had a red cover. I could only see the edge of it. Then some guy lit a cigarette and I had to go outside the shelter."

Polly's hopes begin to warm up again; Jane seems willing to talk to her, one person to another, with a certain amount of warm interest. Most of the time, that is. Sometimes the mercury drops on the Jane side of the living room, and Polly cannot figure out what provokes this. She's stopped asking; it only makes things worse.

Polly returns to her narrative and explains that the library locale has two forms of move-along guards. The ones belonging to the library are benign for the most part. The street folk were tolerated as long as they didn't importune patrons for money or block the doorways, at which time they were gently shooed away by an employee in a vest marked "Security". Polly suspects the librarians take turns wearing it.

The other kind, employed by the bus company, is what the crime novels term rent-a-cops. "Not nice people," in Polly's book.

"When the weather's bad, like it is today, everyone just crams into any shelter they can find. I gave up and went back in the shelter, and then a bunch of other people came down the steps. I guess the library police shooed them away from the doorway again. They all tramped down to where I'm sitting, turned away from the smoker, diving into my book."

"And trying not to miss your bus, like that other time."

"Right. So our library hooker is crammed in there too. She's reading a mangy-looking old hardback, you know, like libraries retire from circulation and sell five for a dollar at their tent sale. You could still see an old property stamp on the side of the pages like they used to do."

"So did you manage to figure out what she was reading?"

"Steinbeck."

"Huh."

"So up struts one of those bus company cop guys, shooing those poor folks out into the rain. And this guy is just, I dunno, he's belligerent, bellicose, and downright nasty. People don't move fast enough for him so he just starts grabbing them and shoving them out in the rain. Our hooker shoves her book into her jacket; it's not much of a jacket anyway, skimpy fake-fur thing, but she's trying to keep her book dry. He grabs her sleeve and just yanks, hard, you know?"

"Oh, Polly, what did you do?" Polly, despite her focus on the day's events, feels a certain thrill at hearing her name come from Jane's lips. It's been so long

"Nothing, at that point. I'm sitting there all white and middle-class, feeling guilty because I'm in out of the rain. But then she dropped her book, it just missed a big puddle, and that...man snatched it up. He started accusing her of stealing 'public property' from the library. That's when I stood up."

"Uh, oh."

"I said, 'Excuse me.' He looked at me, honest to God, his jaw hung down, just hung there, and he said, 'Huh?' "

Excuse me," repeats Polly, "But that's actually my book. I just checked it out and I'm lending it to, uh, Rose here."

"Huh?" says the troglodyte again. "Huh? Why would you do that?"

"We're in the same book group. Here at the library. Rose forgot her library card today so we checked it out on my card. See? This is my card. That I used to check out Grapes of Wrath. That's this month's selection."

"Same book group, huh? You and her?" His face is a study in derision, swinging between the two women. "So, what did you read last time?"

The prostitute looks straight at her accuser, deadpan, and says nothing.

"Carrie."

"Huh?

"Carrie. A novel by Stephen King.

"Okay," he turns to the prostitute, "What was that one about? That Carrie one?"

'Rose' is gleeful. "It's an earlier work by King, about a teenage girl with telekinesis."

Polly notices that 'Rose' has no trouble with the word 'telekinesis'.

'Rose' continues, "She uses it to get revenge on her tormenters."

Polly chimes in helpfully, "This months' selection is a further examination of the persecution of the downtrodden in America." 'Rose' smirks at that.

The rent-a-cop thrusts the book back at Polly, who hands it to 'Rose'. "Well, you just make sure you return it to the library on time. I wouldn't trust 'Rose' here (he sneers, just like, Polly thinks, a villain in one of those old melodramas) not to hock it somewhere.

"But did he let her keep it?" asks Jane.

"Yeah, he did. I was afraid he'd march us both into the library to confirm the story but I guess he had to move to the next stop to bother the folks there."

"Did you at least find out her real name?"

"My bus came. I just said, 'see you', and she said, 'Hey, thanks', and that was that.

"ROSE, HUH?"

"Oh!"

"Sorry. Didn't mean to scare you. Thought you saw me come up."

"No, I guess I was immersed. I haven't seen you around lately."

'Rose' grins. "Lunchtime business has been pretty active lately. Weather got better. Hey, I wanted to thank you for fronting that dude."

"Fronting?"

"Facing him down. You know, about the book. So hey, what's that name mean, 'Rosasharn' or however you say it?"

"I think they were saying 'Rose of Sharon' in an Oklahoma accent. You know, like those shrubs in people's yards that bloom in August. What is your name, really?"

"La-Christine.

"La-Christine? Very exotic.

"Real name was LaKesha. But it's Christine now. My working name, you know?"

"I like LaKesha," offers Polly, but Christine wrinkles her nose.

"You know how many LaShawnas, LaToyas, LaKeshas, and LaTanyas lived on my block when I was coming up? They all dropped out of school by the time they were sixteen."

"Oh," says Polly, at a loss.

"Course, Christine didn't exactly graduate either. I only lack two courses for a GED if I could just—"

"Why don't you get yourself...." But Christine has walked away. "...a library card?" Polly finishes lamely. A car has slid up to the curb near the bus stop; the passenger window rolls down and Christine leans in. A moment later she hops into the car; as the car drives away, she wiggles her fingers 'goodbye' to Polly.

"I thought she seemed a little sheepish as she left," Polly tells Jane, "But maybe I imagined it."

Jane thinks for a minute. "Suppose she knows about the GED prep program? Bet the library has brochures about it. You should ask her."

POLLY'S NOW A CONFIRMED MASS transit commuter, and she likes it that way. Even the worst weather lends punctuation to her days, sharpens her senses.

"Hey, I got an idea," Polly says, pushing the front door closed behind her. Jane, in her office corner, looks up from her computer screen but it's not an interested look. Polly thinks it's more of an "I'll listen if I have to, but not happily" look.

"What," says Jane, belatedly.

"Never mind, it's not important."

"Okay." Jane returns to her screen, that double line between her brows more pronounced than usual.

Polly, discouraged, begins to turn away and mind her own affairs. But no, she decides. "Hey, what's wrong, Jane? You look worried or upset or something."

"Yeah, kinda, but it's just one of those work things. You don't wanna hear about it."

"Sure, I do."

"Really? Jane raises an eyebrow cynically, pulling the double lines a bit askew.

"Well, yeah." Polly hopes she doesn't sound as defensive as she feel. "Why wouldn't I?"

"You don't usually. You say 'huh' and then start talking about your own stuff."

"I do not! Do I?"

"Yep. For the last year or more."

Polly looks more closely at Jane. Jane's lip gives a little quiver, and she swallows. When did Jane get those little eyebrow lines and that slump to her shoulders?

"Oh, Jane. I'm so sorry. You seem so strong, so in charge of everything, I never thought you needed me to... to... you know."

"Well, it sure would be nice to have someone act like they give a shit once in a while."

"Oh, honey. I give lots of shits." She leans over and gives Jane a clumsy, one-armed squeeze. Jane leans against Polly for a moment and then emits a sound that's half a sob, half a snort.

"Lots of shits, huh?"

"Yes. Lots. And so tell me about it."

"Oh, it's that rat-bastard Sullivan. You remember, the self-appointed King of the Art Department, who never gives us specs and then bitches when he gets what he didn't ask for?"

"Yeah, the rat-bastard. What did he do today?"

Polly pulls up a footstool, sits down, and listens

*

"GIRL, WHY ARE YOU MAKIN' that noise?" Christine is annoyed. The wind is blustery, straight out of the north, and Polly suddenly realizes that she's the most warmly dressed person at the bus stop. She'd been humming bits of "Just An Old Fashioned Love Song".

"Oops, sorry. Just feeling, you know, kind of mushy."

"Huh?"

"About my sweetie. Jane."

"Yeah, just 'cause you're feelin' mushy (Christine does air quotes) doesn't mean you have to make that noise at everybody."

"Okay, okay, I'll just be mushy in silence."

"Yeah. Can't all of us have a good thing at home. You keep it to yourself, hear?"

"I said okay, jeez."

Christine's shoulders drop. She turns to face Polly.

"I thought I had someone like that for a while. He was fine, you know?"

Polly nods.

"Got me a kid from him. Little Jaxson is five, now. He's with my sister. The other Jaxson, I don't know where he is."

"I'm really sorry. I hope you find someone fine again. You seem pretty fine yourself, you know?"

"Bullshit," says Christine, and saunters away down the sidewalk. Polly doesn't see her for the next week.

"CHRISTINE! HEY, HOW ARE YOU doing?" Polly tries not to notice the puffy contusion on Christine's cheekbone.

"How you think I'm doin? You see my face? I'd doing like garbage, that's how."

"Yeah, I see. Sucks, I guess."

"'I guess,'" Christine mocks bitterly

Polly thinks about how her talk with Jane went, how it helped them both for Polly to just listen. It was a new experience for both, and it felt good.

"Do you want to tell me about it?"

"No."

Well. That was definite enough.

Polly doesn't push her further. "What I was going to say can wait for a better time, maybe."

"Naw, that's okay. What is it?

"It's about your GED. Jane and I were talking—"

"Jane? You're telling my business to other people? Who told you you could do that, huh?"

Polly pulls back, eyes wide. "Jane's not 'other people'! She's my girlfriend! My friends are her friends, is all."

"I ain't your friend. Who says I'm your friend?"

"Well, I thought we were book friends. I'm sorry; I'll leave you alone if you want." Polly takes a step back, bumping against the fire hydrant that stands near the bus shelter.

"Well, that's okay, I guess," says Christine, settling her shoulders inside her fake fur jacket. "What were you talking about to, uh, Jane?"

"Jane worked with someone who tutored people for the GED. That was when she lived in Duluth—"

"Girl, get to the point. I gotta get to work. My boss is mad at me as it is."

"Ok, Jane says the libraries have tutors, or can find tutors, and provide textbooks and stuff you need for it. All you need is a library card."

"I had one. Then they started this 'yearly card renewal' shit and I didn't have a good address any more to give 'em. My sister threw me out, and she doesn't live in town any more, and hell, what's the use...."

"Maybe we can—"

"We? What's this 'we'? Ain't no 'we' in this thing."

Polly opens her mouth, but sees Christine's face and stops.

"Naw, I ain't got time for this now."

Christine turns and walks away without a farewell. Polly, thinking of the bruise, doesn't take the brusque departure personally. She thinks about how to organize an address for Christine. Or how to invent one.

"Yo."

"Oh, hi, Christine. How are you?"

"Ooooh, somebody done got up on the wrong side of the dirt this morning, looks like."

"Not me. Jane."

"Jane? Your girlfriend?"

"Sometimes. Lately I wonder. I think she wants to break up. Just when I was thinking things were getting better, they weren't!"

"She messing around with someone else? Got a little somp'n outside?"

"What? No!"

"She knock you around?"

"No!"

"Doesn't sound like you got anythin' to complain about, then."

"She's mad at me and I don't know why."

"Aw, that's bullshit. If she mad at you, you gotta have an idea why. You messing around with someone else?"

"No! I think it's because the roof is leaking, but I didn't make it that way!" Polly realizes she's whining like a three-year-old.

"How long have you been rentin' there? Maybe she needs you to pay more rent but doesn't know how to say? I had a landlord like that. 'Course, come to find out he was really wantin' something else.

"Oh, I don't pay rent. We own the house together."

"How much does the roofer want to fix it? Maybe she's upset about that. Maybe she's worried you won't pay your share?"

"I don't know how much it costs. She didn't tell me. She just kept changing the buckets under the drips and getting more mad."

"How come she needs to tell you how much? Didn't you both talk to the roofer? How many buckets did you empty? "

"I don't know if she's even called a roofer yet. And she never told me I needed to change any buckets!"

"How come she needs to call the roof man? Your phone broke? Your arms broke you can't empty your share of buckets?"

"No, she just always…."

"Girl, I'd be mad too! You need to step up there, do your share! You ain't no child."

"Now you sound just like her.

"I take that as a compliment, sounds like Jane doesn't need to be a babysitter for some grown woman."

"Yeah, yeah, I get the point." And she does.

"Hey, honey. Sorry I'm late; I got caught up on the phone and missed the five-fifteen bus. I've been trying to call you, but I couldn't get through."

"Did you give my number to those Desert Dry Roofing people?"

"Oh, did they call already? Damn! I wanted to check with you first. Yeah, I've been looking up roofers, reading reviews, you know."

"You have, huh? What got you doing that?"

"Well, you were pretty upset about the leak, and I guess I didn't realize that I was too, until later when I couldn't stop thinking about it.

"You couldn't?"

"Well, it's my leak too, isn't it?"

"Uh, yeah?"

"Did those roofers seem okay to you?"

Jane shakes her head, clearly taken aback, but then nods. "Seemed okay to me," she concedes.

"So, let's find a time we'll both be here when they can come out. Did they say if they do evenings?"

Bemused, Jane pulls up her calendar and sits down next to Polly. If both of them feel a subtle warmth between their barely touching arms, neither of them mentions it.

"Hey, girl."

"Christine! Hey! I got an idea about the library card!"

Christine sighs, the long, weary sound of a mother with one too many importunate children. "What's your big idea?"

"You just need an official ID with your picture on it, and something official that shows your address, right?"

"Yeah, still got my school ID, but it's expired."

"They might not care about that, as long as your address is current. So, hey, what if we sent something to my address with your name—"

"Girl, what did I say about this 'we' shit? Huh? Huh?"

Polly shrinks back. The woman (white) in the bus shelter looks at them. Christine looks at the woman, who hurriedly opens her purse and roots around in it aimlessly. Christine turns the lasers back to Polly.

"Sorry," whispers Polly

"You better say 'sorry'. I don't need no Karen to tell me how to do my business, you hear? You go be Lady Bountiful on someone else, okay?"

"Lady Bountiful? No way, Christine. It's, you know, women help other women. You help me and I help you…."

"I'll get that certificate in my own way, in my own time, hear? Huh? You hear me?

"I hear you. But...."

Christine has turned on her heel and strides briskly away.

"Try to help some people," says the white woman, sympathetically.

"Oh, shut up," comes to Polly's lips, but doesn't escape them. She's not sure who "Karen" is, but she knows she doesn't want to be her. She bets Karen isn't a lesbian.

"Hey, Christine," ventures Polly, timidly.

"Hey, girl."

Christine doesn't sound angry anymore, so Polly jumps right in. "I know this makes you mad, and I don't know why, but I know how readers feel when they can't get their hands on books they want, and if it were me I'd want you to jump in and help me if you could, so I'm just going to say this...."

Christine gives her an unbelieving stare, but doesn't storm away, so Polly continues at auctioneer pace, "I give you my address and you send something addressed to your name, at my address. When I get it in the mail I give it to you, you show it to the librarians with your ID, and then they send the library card to you at my address, and I give that to you. Done. You don't ever have to speak to me again, but you'll have the card to do whatever you want with."

Christine tosses her head back, gives a little foxlike bark. The nacre insets of her dangly earrings catch the cold sunlight and give back tiny rainbows.

"You got your nerve, going on about that."

Polly looks up under her brows. "I know." It comes out as a whisper.

"Okay. Gimme your address."

"Really?"

"Don't push me. Just gimme that damn address."

Polly scribbles on the back of a CVS receipt and passes it to Christine, who takes it haughtily, turns her back, and walks away.

Polly still wonders who Karen is, but thinks she won't ask Christine that for a long time. If ever.

"Hey, look! I'm home when I expected to be! All the buses were running on…

"Who's LaKesha Williams?"

Polly looks at the envelope in Jane's hand and tries to keep her shoulders from rising toward her ears. She can tell it isn't working.

"Uh, that's Christine."

"Christine?"

"From the library."

"The hooker? Why are we getting a hooker's mail sent to our house?"

"She's not a… well, I guess she is a… what you said. But she's my book friend too, you know."

"Okay, I get that. But, why? Why. Are. We. Getting…. your book friend's mail at our house? She moving in?"

"Don't be mad. I'm just helping her out. She needs an address. You know, for the library."

"No, I don't know."

"I told you. You and I've had library cards for so long we forget how it works. You need proof of a mailing address, and some ID, to get a card in the first place. She can show them this letter, along with her old student photo ID, and they'll mail her card here. Then I'll give it to her and that will be that."

"And when her… customers start showing up here? Polly, I don't appreciate your—"

"Why would anybody show up here? That doesn't make any sense; only the library will see this envelope! Jane, I'm sorry if this upsets you, really I am. But I'm glad she can get her card now. Hey! Give it back! Give!"

Jane gives up her move to tear the letter. Reluctantly, she hands it to Polly. "If anybody shows up here, Polly…."

"We'll both be really upset, yeah, I get it. But you know, I bet nobody does. C'mon, Jane, you'd want to help her out too, if you knew her."

"Well, since she reads Steinbeck...."

"I knew you would," grins Polly.

"Hey, Christine! Over here!"

Christine, clearly occupied in business negotiations, shakes her head at Polly. Polly, impatient, waves an envelope.

"It came!"

"Girl, shut up! I'm busy here...aw, naw, hey, man...shit!" The car drives away. Christine turns on her 5-inch heel and clicks away down the sidewalk

"No, wait! Just let me give you this..." Polly breaks into a run, but Christine keeps walking, eyes resolutely ahead.

"Damn!" mutters Polly, and turns back to the bus stop. Just in time, too, as the number 17 pulls up to the curb.

"Polly, man, you gotta pay attention. When I'm trying to get a customer, you gotta not interrupt me. You scare them off, and I'm out some money."

"I know," sighs Polly, "I'm sorry. No, wait! Why am I apologizing to you? I was doing you a favor!"

"Some favor," sniffs Christine, "I told you about favors. I don't need no favors."

"I got Jane mad at me again for this! So here. Do whatever you want with it."

"What is it?" Christine's tone is grudging.

"That library card that came to my address yesterday. That you applied for, using the letter that came to my address, remember? The library card you need to get books for your classes?"

"Oh, hey, right." She takes the official library envelope and looks down at it, smoothing the surface with her thumbs. "You know, I didn't really believe it would work."

"Well, it did. Now you have it. Guess you'd better get back to work now. I know I have to."

"Hey, no. Hey, this is great, you know?" She huffs out a brief laugh and then begins to carefully peel open the envelope flap. Despite herself, Polly lingers to watch. The flap gives way easily and Christine pulls out the cover letter. The plastic card adheres to the lower corner; Christine pulls it away.

"What do they use to stick this on here? Looks like snot."

"Gross!" says Polly, and they both laugh, a little shakily.

Christine looks up from the card. "You gotta get to work, remember?"

"Yeah, I know. So, you know, you can go in there any time now and start picking out whatever books you want. No more discards for the brilliant LaKesha Christine Williams!"

"I can't hardly believe it. Don't tell anybody, but," Christine lowers her voice, "I'm a little nervous about going in there. Got used to bein chased off."

"Hey, you have to get to work too. If you don't get into the library by next week, wait for me at the regular time and we'll go in together."

"Girl, who you talking to? I can't wait a whole week. I'm going in there today!" She squares her shoulders and looks up at the venerable library façade as though sizing up a trick. Polly gives a brief wave and walks back to the bus stop.

*

POLLY ALIGHTS FROM THE NUMBER 17 bus and looks around. No Christine. At work, maybe. Polly tries not to picture her friend "at work" and trots up the stairs to the library entrance.

She stops in the lobby, blinks. Christine is at the checkout desk, book in hand. It's funny, Polly thinks, how bashful it makes you feel when you see someone you know, in a different environment. Your high school teacher at the pharmacy, or a co-worker at a restaurant. Or your streetwise book friend, actually checking out a book at the library. Should she approach? She slides a foot forward, then the other, and eventually sidles up to the desk in a hangdog, "Aw shucks" manner.

"Polly! How you doing? What are you reading these days?"

Polly blinks again. Shyly, she holds up her Nevada Barr mystery. "Still working on this series. What do you… oh, more Steinbeck! That's a really sad one."

"It's on the best literature list for the program."

"You can check out several of the books on the list at the same time, you know," volunteers the librarian.

"I only have room to carry one book at a time," Christine says.

"I can give you a bag," persists the librarian.

Polly reads her friend's mounting annoyance and speaks up. "She's a, uh, delivery person. You know, like a courier. Travels light?"

"Yeah. Courier. This one book for now."

"Suit yourself," says the librarian. "Who'd have thought it?" she says in her head, noting Christine's colorful ensemble, but hey, the woman has a valid library card and the librarian quite enjoys supplying an obvious streetwalker with Of Mice and Men.

CHRISTINE STROLLS OVER TO THE bus stop when she sees Polly step down from the bus. Without preamble, she says, "You were right. That was a reeealy sad story. I sure never expected that cowboy to shoot his own friend. Yow!"

"What are you reading next?"

"1984. About the end times, a bit, but without the religion. I remember Brave New World was like that, but it was more upbeat."

"You talk differently when we're talking about books, did you notice?"

"Did I notice? Who you talkin' to?" Polly isn't sure whether she's offended the woman, but at her hesitation Christine relents. "You talkin' to one a those lizards."

"How's that?"

"Oh, you know, those lizards that change color when they on a green or a brown leaf. Chameleon?"

"Chameleon, right. How are you one of those?"

"When you were little and you looked in a mirror, what color did you see?"

"Well, white, I guess."

"Nuh-uh. No, you didn't notice at all. No white child looks in the mirror and says 'Look at that! I'm white!' And no child who's not white does either, at first. But she soon does, before she even goes to school. She studies that color. 'Am I lighter than Stell? Darker than that new girl in the pew in front of me?' And that child learns to talk and act differently wherever she is, depending on who she's talking to."

"I guess you would," mused Polly.

"We learn it waaaay early. Have to. Like that chameleon, it's a survival thing."

"Huh. Guess it would have to be. Have fun with Orwell."

"Who?"

"Your book."

"Oh, yeah. I already forgot what I had. Well..." Christine tucks her paperback into the pocket of her leopard-fur jacket and sashays off to her regular corner, waving vaguely back at Polly. Clearly, she has switched back into work mode.

THREE WEEKS LATER. POLLY HASN'T seen Christine at all. Winter is seriously closing in, and Polly has no idea how a prostitute can make a living at outdoor work that entails flimsy clothing and customers idling slowly around in cars in the snow and ice. She hopes there's a more protected version of the profession.

She asks the librarian at the checkout desk, "Have you seen my friend lately? The one who was in a couple of weeks ago getting books on the GED prep list?"

"The pros...uh, you mean the tall colorful woman? How's she doing with the program?"

"That's the problem, I don't know. I haven't seen her in all that time. Maybe I shouldn't worry...."

"No, I'm sorry. Haven't seen her. If I do, I'll tell her someone was looking for her."

"That would be good, thanks. Tell her Polly's starting to worry."

"I will." The woman scribbles on a sticky note. Polly squints at the upside-down writing.

"Street w-Polly". Good enough.

The fourth Wednesday, Polly comes in the front door and stands, keys hanging from her hand, head down as though studying an invisible piece of navel piercing.

"Working out the answer to the world's problems?"

"Oh! Jane. I didn't see you there."

"Ah. Christine not there again, huh?"

"Right. The librarian hasn't seen her. They said she has a book that's due, but not to worry if she's having a problem. I don't know what that means." But Polly does.

Her voice shakes but she continues, "I even asked some of the folks around the bus shelter, the few that are still out in the weather, anyway. Nobody has seen her." Polly's eyes fill with tears. "One guy told me, he said…"

"What?" Jane puts an arm around Polly's shoulders.

"He said, 'Girls like that disappear, they working a new corner. Or they dead.' Oh, Jane! Should I call the police?"

"I have an idea they wouldn't be much help. Maybe they would. But maybe…oh, hell! I don't know. I'm sorry, Poll, I don't know enough to guess what might be going on. Maybe all you can do is wait."

"Wait for what?"

"Better weather? Oh, Polly, don't. I'm sorry, hon. So, so sorry." They hold each other and rock as Polly weeps, and after a bit, so does Jane.

"Hi, Sweetie!"

Jane doesn't know what has cheered Polly up, but she's glad for whatever it is. "What are you looking all twinkly about?"

"What about a new roof?"

"Get out! What, Polly, you won the lottery?"

"Nope. I just decided something when I was sitting at the bus stop today. I'm not going to buy a car. We can use the insurance check to pay for the roof."

"It's a great idea, except for one little catch. You can't drive a roof, Polly."

"No, but the bus works pretty well for most things, and I can take one of those ride-share things for other places. When we go places together maybe I can pay for part of the gas when you drive? Or pay for the ride-share for both of us. Lots cheaper than keeping two cars, and we can have a roof, too."

"Pretty clever. "

"I thought so," says Polly happily. Jane notices this is the first time Polly has smiled in nearly a month. She realizes she's feeling damned cheerful herself. Silently, she thanks Christine, wherever she may be. Christine, somehow, has turned things around in their household.

"You are not going to believe what came in the mail today."

"What's that...oh!"

"Yeah. Looks like it's been through the mill, and I guess she didn't know your last name, but it found its way here."

"Open it, please. I can't stand it."

Jane rips open the grubby envelope and pulls out the note; a library card falls to the floor. Polly reaches for it as though it's a talisman and lifts it using both hands. She holds it to her chest as Jane reads:

"Hey, girl.

Sorry I didn't tell you I was going away but I got in a hurry.

I've gone over to Illinois with little Jaxson to stay with my sister. She says we can stay while I finish the GED and get some indoor work, ha ha. I've still got one more unit to do but I know I can do it no problem.

Hey, thanks Polly for helping me get going on this. At first, I thought you were doing one of those "liberal white ladies to the rescue" thing and it really pissed me off, you know?

But after a while, when you kept calling us "book friends" I saw that you were just helping out, like anybody would. Women help other women, right?

I got a new library card here, so would you take that one back to them and tell them I'll send back that last book when I find an envelope the right size.

Your educated book friend,

Rose"

"Wow."

"Yeah." Jane wipes a tear away and suggests, "Let's go out to dinner, honey. We have a lot to celebrate."

When I first moved to a new city, of course one of my first stops was at the library. I was impressed by the variety of people who hung out around the library. My first thought was, "Wow, this is some literate town where even the hookers find a home at the library!"

THE OTHER WOMAN

From: sgralying85@gmail.com
To: Chiquita.Crombie@sanjose.edu
Subject: Updates from back East

Hey Chic-

    You about settled in there? Man, when I grew up I figured I'd buy myself a house and stay in one place and make friends and we'd all grow old together in the same town. Now there you are way the hell out on the coast and yeah, I know, I know, we'll still be friends 4-ever. But I sure do miss your old ass. Well, not your actual ass, LOL.

    But that was one helluva party wasn't it? Had to laf thinking of you with the momma of all hangovers, climbing on that plane with Squiggy howling in her carrier.

    Things have been pretty quiet around here. Went to Patty and Meg's house for euchre (had to look up how to spell that, LOL) the other nite. Good thing we don't play for real money. :)

    Are your students there any better than the ones you had here? Hah.

    Well back to work for me,

    -Stace-

*

From: sgralying85@gmail.com
To: Chiquita.Crombie@sanjose.edu
Subject: Re: Updates from back East

Chic-

Didn't mean to whine about you moving. Really, we're all getting along fine here. Well, fine as we ever are. Carla come over night before last, drunk on her ass again. She told Sally to f*ck off, about time I told her but you know how she is, before you know it she'll find someone else to mess around with. I don't know why Teresa puts up with Carla's carrying on.

Potluck tomorrow nite. I thot about making that cabbage thing you do but guess I'll pick up a box of Kentucky Fried. Don't know where you find the time to do all that great cooking.

-Stace-

*

From: sgralying85@gmail.com
To: Chiquita.Crombie@sanjose.edu
Subject: Re: Re: Updates from back East

Whats up Chic-man,

Potluck was about the same as usual. Saw some of the same old same old and some I haven't seen for a long time. Carla and Teresa were there. Teresa had another black eye—everyone saw it and pretended they dint. Maybe that's why she puts up with the cheating, Carla's nicer to her then?

Hey, you'll never guess who else showed up. "Thank you Daddy", remember? LOL. Yeah, they're still together but not hanging all over each other anymore.

Gotta go, I'm on call tomorrow starting early.

-Stace-

PS you still loving that new job? Who are your new pals? Not a bunch of professors I hope.

*

From: sgralying85@gmail.com
To: Chiquita.Crombie@sanjose.edu
Subject: Re: Why did I do this?

The lovebirds did it again! Yeah, I can't believe I keep falling for that. Bunch of old matchmakers, jeez. "Come on over for dinner, we made too much pot roast". Hah. Come to find out, Joann's cousin over in Mayville broke up with her girlfriend so Joann called HER (the cousin, not the ex-girlfriend LOL), right, because she made too much pot roast!!! This one wasn't all spiritual, anyway, but wow. All the cousin, I can't even remember her name, it's Madeline or Madison or something, knows anything about is shit she's seen on TV. I go, "I don't watch TV", and she goes, "Really? Wow. Hey, did you see on American Idol the other night?" And I go, "I don't watch TV", and she goes, "Yeah, you said. Hey, did you see ——-???"

Shit, man, I can't believe you can't find a house. I was thinking you'd get rich, moving to that high-powered job on the coast. You mean even with the housing bust you still have to pay that much for a house out there? Wow.

Good thing you left all the big stuff at your folks. If you had to pay storage!

Maybe you can get a fixer-upper and I can fly out there and help you fixer-upper, LOL. Remember that time I "fixed" the bathtub faucet and it went a gusher in the closet? And that's when I found out the shutoff valve dint work? ROTFLMAO! But not so funny then.

-Stace-

*

From: sgralying85@gmail.com
To: Chiquita.Crombie@sanjose.edu
Subject: This and that

I don't even know if I was serious about helping you with the house. Maybe I could. I do have some vacation coming, just haven't felt like going anywhere lately. Let me know if you DO decide to get that "dive" (hey, I thot it looked okay in the picture anyway) and what you think needs to be done to it. You know I'm okay with electrical and pretty good with drywall anyway. And I can handle a paintbrush pretty good too. Better get someone else for plumbing, LOL.

You know how we always said Teresa would never change and neither would Carla? Well, get this. Meg and Patty threw a birthday party for Teresa. (Carla got drunk and pretty mouthy before it was all over, but what else is new.) Turns out Meg remembered Teresa used to have a mess of horse pictures back before Carla tore up all her albums. So Meg gives Teresa a free riding lesson at one of the stables out near them, and says she'll spend a whole morning driving around with her to pick out the one she likes best.

You know how Teresa is when Carla's around, how she never takes her eyes off Carla so she can laf when Carla does and look mad when Carla does and all that? It was amazing, Chic, she just completely ignored Carla and her face just glowed. She goes, "This weekend?" And Meg goes, "Sure, if you want. We'll spend all Saturday morning or until you decide on a place."

Carla was pretty pissed about THAT idea, you can bet. She goes, "No can do, babe. We're going bowling Saturday morning."

And guess what? T goes right ahead and says, "No, if Meg's going to do this for me, I'm going. It's what I've wanted to do, like, forever." Man, Carla was pissed, but Teresa just acted like she dint even notice. Bet Carla whacks her, and she changes her mind in a hurry. Sucks, huh?

Let me know about that house and I'll see what I can do about getting away.

-Stace the ever-helpful-

*

From: sgralying85@gmail.com
To: Chiquita.Crombie@sanjose.edu
Subject: This and that

Sorry that house deal fell through. Keep looking, man, anything's better than paying all that rent. Poor Squiggy, does she hate that apartment? I'd piss in the corners too if I got stuck somewhere I hated, LOL.

No, I haven't seen Joann's cousin again, are you crazy? Told you I'm not looking. I have a good time by myself most of the time, and with pals. Yeah, I miss you a lot too.

Oh, Carla came over last Sunday, not as drunk as usual, bitching up a storm about Teresa. She goes, "That bitch has signed up for these damned expensive riding lessons *every Saturday*. She knows we can't afford that kind of shit."

Good for Teresa, huh? Remember back when we'd all hang out at The Jewel Box every weekend, and Carla would spend half her paycheck getting plowed and putting ten-dollar bills in the drag queen's cleavage? That time when she got so blasted, she puked all over her boots, and Teresa nearly cried? Come to find out, those were Teresa's boots, she'd had them from when she was going to get a horse but somehow, she ended up with bitchy old Carla instead.

Anyway, it makes me want to go out and watch Teresa bounce around on a stupid horse, just so I can cheer for her.

Going out to dinner with Meg and Patty on Saturday. Not much else going on here.

-Stace-

*

From:	sgralying85@gmail.com
To:	Chiquita.Crombie@sanjose.edu
Subject:	My kingdom for a ?

Yeah, Teresa's still taking the riding lessons. Carla's still pissed about it. But no more black eyes that I can see. Wonders never cease :)

Damn, that place on my roof is leaking, *again*. How many times have we tried to fix that? Anyway, you weren't here to hold the ladder so this time I got up in the attic and crawled around forever and found it! It's way over toward the front, where that vent is up on the peak? The water comes in around that and runs along the beam at the peak, and then down another joist, and stops right above the light fixture. Sherlock Holmes strikes again, LOL. I climbed up on the roof anyway, no I did NOT fall on my ass, and put a bunch of that roof-patch goop around the vent and it's okay for now. Do you get autumn rains out there too?

Having any luck on the house hunt? Just seems like with all the stuff for sale right now you'd have lots to choose from.

Ran into Sally at the Lowes when I was getting the goop for the roof. We're going to the film festival tomorrow nite. She's good people. I don't know why she wanted to mess with Carla in the first place. She says she didn't realize what was going on at first, thot she was pals with both of them, but T wasn't around much. Or some dumb thing. Maybe I believe her.

-Stace-

*

From:	sgralying85@gmail.com
To:	Chiquita.Crombie@sanjose.edu
Subject:	Those damn holidays

Yo, Chic.

What did you decide to do about Thxgiving? I know your folks would be soooo happy to see you (yah, I'm <u>still</u> jealous of your parents and the great relationship you guys have) :). I'll be going to the community gig and help serve, like I always do. It's kind of fun. Then, I'll just go home and crash the rest of the weekend. Maybe take in a show with Sally. No, it's not like that, we just hang out.

-Stace-

*

From:	sgralying85@gmail.com
To:	Chiquita.Crombie@sanjose.edu
Subject:	Re: Those damn holidays

I survived Dinner with the Widows and Orphans, LOL. Well, not completely widows and orphans, a few couples were there too. Carla and Teresa, can you believe that? C was NOT happy about being there. She goes, "SHE didn't have time for cooking this year. SHE had to spend the morning with The Other Woman."

I was pretty surprised, you can imagine, what other woman? But T didn't even look scared like she usually does when Carla's pissed. She just went, "Honey, you could have put the turkey in the oven while I was with Queenie." I didn't notice any bruises on her. Carla's really getting mellow in her old age.

Yah, I get you, better to wait for Xmas to fly back and see your folks. Let me know when you make your plans. I can pick you up at the airport if you want and drop you at your folks.

-S-

*

From: sgralying85@gmail.com
To: Chiquita.Crombie@sanjose.edu
Subject: Lookin for a home

Well, that one house didn't sound too bad, the one with the patio. Have you made an offer on it or still shopping around?

Are those college kids any smarter after a holiday break?

Oh, I forget to tell you that, didn't I? No, Teresa doesn't really have an actual girlfriend. Queenie is that horse Teresa rides all the time, Carla calls her The Other Woman. Man, the way Teresa talks about that animal, though, she acts like it's a girlfriend. It's about all she can talk about. I almost feel sorry for Carla; she just follows along behind her looking crabby.

The lovebirds tried to fix me up again, but I outfoxed them this time. They're like "Come on over for dinner, we made lots." And I'm like, "OK if I bring a date?" Laf! Their faces just fell. They must have had another cousin to get rid of.

Sally and I went to the potluck. I was telling her about that great cabbage thing you used to make but she says she doesn't like cabbage much, so we took that famous lesbian green bean thing with the mushroom soup. Quit making that face, Chic! LOL!

-Stace-

＊

From: sgralying85@gmail.com
To: Chiquita.Crombie@sanjose.edu
Subject: Christmas is a-comin

Yo, Chic-o-la!

You're really coming for xmas, how cool is that? Tell me when you know your flight number, times, yadda yadda, and I'll be at the Arrivals pull-in with reindeer bells on

Gonna plan a party while you're here so you hafta tell me when's good for you. Talk to your folks and let me know asap so I can scrape the mold off the kitchen counter LOL.

I told Sally you were coming and she said she's looking forward to seeing you again. I guess you guys dint hang out together much, did you?

-Stace the reindeer-

*

From: sgralying85@gmail.com
To: Chiquita.Crombie@sanjose.edu
Subject: You know!

Wow, Chiquita. I sure didn't expect THAT. Guess you dint realize I felt that way too, huh? Hell, I didn't know it myself and that's the truth.

Poor Sally, I kept thinking all the time whether I could get serious about her, and the answer kept being 'Nah', but I dint know why. Or why I felt this big empty feeling in the pit of my stomach when you moved so far away. I just thought it was 'cause we've been best friends for so long.

And what's so cool is that we're still best friends, aren't we? Just with, you know, this new stuff on top.

I don't even worry about where this is gonna go, you know? I just feel so rich and happy right now. Course I'll want to come out and see you whenever it works out for us both. I can help you fix up your place, wherever that turns out to be.

Luvya,
-Stacey-

*

From: sgralying85@gmail.com
To: Chiquita.Crombie@sanjose.edu
Subject: Life's good

Chic, don't worry, I'm not going to sit at home and mope, and don't you do that either. I'm going to the potluck this weekend and check up on what everybody's been up to over the holidays. Good thing I didn't get around to throwing that party, huh?

Your folks are as great as ever. Maybe they wouldn't mind if I stopped by and said 'hi' to them once in a while.

Going back to work sux, specially when there's 18 inches of snow in the driveway. You were smart to move to California even if the housing market stinks.

It sounds like you've found some good people out there, even if they're all crunchy-granola.

Yours,
-Stacey-

*

From: sgralying85@gmail.com
To: Chiquita.Crombie@sanjose.edu
Subject: News around town

Potluck, where do I start? Pam and Mary had a big fight over New Years and kept making poison eyes at each other the whole evening. Yeah, Teresa still has her Queenie fixation. Do you know what "posting" is? She's just full of herself because she's learning how to do it, but I googled it and it's just bouncing around on the horse instead of trying NOT to bounce around. Carla's stopped being mad at her and is just sort of ignoring her. She doesn't seem to have anyone else on the side yet, anyways. Give her time, LOL
-Your Stacey-
How cool is that?

*

From: sgralying85@gmail.com
To: Chiquita.Crombie@sanjose.edu
Subject: Happy ground hog day

Bet spring doesn't pack the same punch when you're out there in Sunny Cal, huh? Guess what? I'm coming out there for the whole week! My boss goes, "Well, if you can get that payables routine fixed before you go..." in that "poor me" way she does, and I go, "Great! I'll have it done and <u>tested</u> too!" I dint tell her it was nearly done anyway, LOL. I'll try to get a flight on Valentine's Day.

We'll see if we can really stand each other then! :)
Love ya,
-Stacey the Valentine Fairy-
No, Groundhog Fairy.
Whatever.

*

From: sgralying85@gmail.com
To: Chiquita.Crombie@sanjose.edu
Subject: Flying in crappy weather

I'm so excited about seeing you tomorrow, but kinda scared too. You know I never did like flying, and these early storms are creeping me out. Gonna fly out in the middle of severe thunderstorms, cross your fingers. I guess the plane gets above the clouds and it's not a big deal then, right?

Anyhoo, flight's due at 3:35 pm YOUR time. Gotta take my swiss army knife out of my carry-on, that sux.
-Stacy the World Traveler-

*

From: sgralying85@gmail.com
To: Chiquita.Crombie@sanjose.edu
Subject: Big decisions, huh?

I don't know, Chic. I could probably find a job out there, but I see what you mean about finding a place you like. Like I said, I'd want to have separate quarters for a while just because we've both seen what happens when people move in together too fast. So we'll have to find TWO places we like, close enuf that we're not driving all the time. Don't want to upset Squiggy any more than she already is, too. Maybe I could just get an apartment in your complex.

Gonna close this down, the tornado sirens went off AGAIN. What a spring! And it's still winter!

-Stace in the basement-

*

From: sgralying85@gmail.com
To: Chiquita.Crombie@sanjose.edu
Subject: From ground zero, nearly.

Dear Chic,

I gave you most of the news when we talked last night, but of course I always think of more stuff after we hang up :(

My place isn't as messed-up as it looked at first. It's just when trees are down all over the neighborhood you start thinking you live in a war zone. The neighbors said the Red Cross even came around with coffee this morning, can you believe that?

Really, your folks place is just fine. The storm dint even go near their part of town.

Love ya,

-Stacey-

*

From: sgralying85@gmail.com
To: Chiquita.Crombie@sanjose.edu
Subject: What a mess

Dear Chic,

Meg just called me. Carla's all freaked out, cause Teresa never came home. She didn't tell anyone like forever because she and Teresa just had an argument and T walked out on her. C thought she might be with one of their friends, but mostly she thought she'd gone out to the horse barn. The stables really got clobbered by the storm, did I mention? I'll call you when I know more.

-Me-

*

From: sgralying85@gmail.com
To: Chiquita.Crombie@sanjose.edu
Subject: Teresa and Queenie.

I know, I still can't believe it either. Shit like this really puts stuff in perspective, you know?

We didn't get the whole story about Teresa before, just what I told you on the phone.

Meg and Patty told me the whole thing while we were sitting Carla's living room and Sally was trying to get her to sleep. I still don't know if it's better or worse, how it all was. I was going to call back and tell you, but I didn't want to cry on the phone. I almost don't want to tell you anyway, but we promised to tell each other everything so here goes.

Everyone thought she might be at the stables when the storm hit, but Andrea, the instructor, hadn't seen her there, and her car wasn't there either. Small wonder, it turns out, cars were smashed up and scattered all over a couple miles, and T's car still isn't found. Lots of the horses were missing, some just wandering around loose, and others buried in wreckage.

Andrea told Carla that they finally found both Teresa and Queenie about a half mile down the road in a ditch, all covered up and beat to shit by the stuff flying around. I didn't ask for details about how beat up, and don't want to know. Enuf to kill a person and a horse, anyway. Teresa's arms were wrapped tight around the horse's neck and Meg says the EMTs had to kind of pull them apart. Gross.

Poor old Carla. Never seemed like they liked each other much, but she's sure torn up. She's paying some guy with a backhoe to dig a hole and bury Queenie. Guess they usually make dog food out of dead horses? Wish I hadn't thought about that.

I put both our names on the flowers. Think I'll make a donation to the animal rescue too.

Funeral's tomorrow, you know that, and I don't want to go, you know that too. Yeah, yeah, I will, and I'll sign both our names. But I hate it.

Love ya,

-Stacey-

*

From: sgralying85@gmail.com
To: Chiquita.Crombie@sanjose.edu
Subject: Awful.

I'm sorry I kept falling apart on the phone. I thot we'd all stand around the funeral home thinking "Serves you right" at Carla, I know that sounds bitchy but all these years of not saying "boo" to her so she wouldn't take it out on Teresa, you get bitchy about it.

What I started to tell you and couldn't get it out, was that one of the pictures they had set up on that table was this blurry one of Teresa and Queenie that Meg took, guess it's the only one anyone bothered taking cause Carla never even saw that horse after all this time. Guess Meg's the only one who ever did, come to think of it.

So Carla saw me looking at the picture, and she came over and just stared at it, tears dripping, while I tried to think of something not too dumb to say. Then she said "I just wish there was anything about me to love as much as she loved that stupid horse." Man. That tears me up.

Love ya,

-Stacey-

No, that's stupid, what I mean is I love you. No lie.

Several times a week, I would leave my happy home to spend a couple of hours with the being whom Harriet jokingly calls "the other woman." Her name is Princess, and when I describe her as 'blond,' it simply means that she has white hair. She has liquid, brown eyes and, despite my happy marriage to Harriet, Princess also has my heart. I have no illusions, however. I think Princess, whose affections lie in her stomach, thinks of me merely as "the carrot lady."

SEND ALL OF
THE INVITATIONS

AFTERNOON BREEZE HAD ALREADY PICKED up.

"Just would start now, before this goddamn skyscraper bridge," I muttered.

I hated heights anyway, and I knew that plenty of these towering coastal bridges had collapsed already. Or, treacherously, partially collapsed. A driver would sail up the approach all unknowing, trying to get a up a head of speed with his ancient balky electric hauler, and just over the rise, howdy! A span would be—not there.

I had seen this first-hand, must have been three years ago. Or four, maybe.

"Hon? Remember that bridge with the missing section? Was it three or four years? St. Pete, was it?" No answer. I was used to this. I didn't take it personally.

Remembering the details of the day, anyway. I wasn't that far behind the blue-green jacked-up truck when its brake lights came on and the tires screamed like a man with his privates in a rat trap. The truck dropped out of sight. I had gotten my CH-MOD stopped, barely, climbed down, tiptoed toward the edge of the great square hole. The last few feet, it must be admitted, I'd dropped to hands and knees and crept to the brink. Sixty feet below, the water sparkled innocently in the sun. Not much breeze that day; I'd heard faint sounds from down there, a little like a lowing cow.

Nothing I could do. I'd backed down the slope, no easy job with the CH-MOD behind me and gone elsewhere.

Now, I rolled up the incline, pulling myself forward over the steering wheel to scan the surface ahead. I grimaced as a side gust gave the MOD a nudge, but we moved steadily forward. Cresting the rise, I relaxed. The roadway continued smooth and evidently solid, obscured only by a clump of palmettoes encroaching on the berm at the bottom. I steered around those when I got there, bumping over the upheaved section of pavement. Several sections, actually; asphalt laid over shifting sands can only hold up for so long.

"It'll hold up as long as we do, I expect," I chuckled. "You okay back there, Hon?" No reply; Honey, nee Marguerite, had been mute since her fever seven years ago. Now and then she'd sigh, a faint rustling whisper, or moan. I had given up trying for more.

Like a burrowing snake, bits of side roads showed through drifts of sand.

"There!" Unnecessarily, I pointed to the left to the remains of an access road. The lightness of the CH-MOD proved its worth on this surface. Bumpy, yes, but it rode easily over the snaking tangles of roots, fallen branches, encroaching clumps of vegetation and upheaved chunks of asphalt. Soon I pulled up at the gatehouse of the Gulf Coast National Seashore.

I was glad to see the gatehouse was still being staffed. The Rangers were an eremitic lot but usually ready to step in when a person needed assistance, and they viewed guardianship of the ancient National Parks system as something holy. I wasn't ever sure why that was; pretty much the entirety of the planet was now preserved and protected from human depredation.

I rolled my window down and held out my pass. The Ranger, engrossed in something in front of him? Her? I wasn't sure, didn't look up. Long hair obscured all of the face save the tip of the nose and a shadow of chin.

"Hello!" I called. No response. "Hey! Do you want to see my pass or don't you?" The Ranger continued his/her study of the open literature—possibly a manual, I thought. "Studying?"

After another moment, I pulled my pass back. "Rude," I muttered, and pulled forward. No shouts of "Halt!" or similar came after us.

The gate bar swung up, whether by auto-sensor or raised by the Ranger didn't really matter to me. I bumped on into the park and swung right into the first parking lot. A few derelict vehicles sagged on shreds of tires, paled nearly white from years of UV and salt air. I parked at the far end of the lot.

"We're here, Hon. Let me get us set up."

There was a time I'd have looked around before exiting the vehicle, on high alert for Marauders. In those days I had almost, though not quite, wished for a small community, even with men, provided they were the right kind, the *safe* kind.

As I stepped down, near-silence folded me close. The wind, blocked to the north by walls of vegetation-crusted sand dunes, was a mere whisper. Outside the bubble of silence was the low-key roar, quiet, roar, quiet of early evening tide waves on the shore. Nary a bird in sight, and of course, no people.

The subaudible wind-water sounds were mournful. Depression muttered at me, "Still here! Ready to quit yet?"

"Shut up," I told it, and got to work.

The CH-MOD (Comprehensive Housing Module, 'MOD for short) was a marvel of engineering; I thought this every time we landed at a new location. Cantilevered roof, walls, screened sides (polyglass sides were stowed underneath), all counterweighted so that I could open a functioning house with one hand. Hand cranks dropped the webbed feet that rode evenly on nearly any sort of surface more solid than quicksand, and the solar covers rolled easily out and hooked over the edges of the eaves. I'd deploy the freestanding solar collectors tomorrow.

Batteries were tucked safely underneath, sealed in their waterproof casings. These batteries, like much of the CH-MOD's amenities, were marvels of Golden Age technology. The surviving scientists around the world, once freed of nationalistic and resource constraints, gleefully collaborated, vying to outdo each other in innovation and utility.

The hose rolled smoothly out; nozzle hooked under my arm, I began the trek to the shoreline. Drifting sand held in place by burgeoning vegetation made the short walk a hike: up one dune, down the other side, squeeze through the buttonwood, croton, sea grape entanglements, curse, repeat, and finally to the smoother sand of the shoreline. Puffing, I tossed the weighted nozzle out as far as I could manage and turned back.

Sand glittered in the slanting rays of the sun. I'd marvel at the beauty of it later, over my evening drink. For now, slog back to the MOD. Nearing eighty, I wondered how much longer I could continue this peripatetic life. Really, there was no further need to keep dodging around. Who was there to stalk, molest, invade us now? The Marauders were either dead or, like aging tomcats, simply past the age of troublemaking. They, too, merely wanted a place in the sun for their declining years.

"Have to see… if Honey's ready… to settle down somewhere," I puffed up the final dune. Leaning against the MOD's side, I leaned down and flipped the switch to the desalinization plant, listened to the *sluuurp!* of air in the hose, replaced by slosh, and finally replaced by a contented mechanical purr as the Gulf water came into the tanks for processing.

"Ready for some fresh air, Hon? Wind's not too bad." Honey rustled faintly as I slid her across the van seat, robe trailing, and settled her into the wheeled lounger. This lounger was also a piece of art, all Cloudfoam padding that rode on all-surface balloon tires, the whole light enough for a child (or a wheezy old broad) to handle but sturdy as well. It glided smoothly down the extension ramp and I turned it to face the shore just as a squadron of pelicans undulated past, angular heads like staples, looking like a collection of pterosaurs rowing through the slanting sun rays.

"Beautiful, huh? Now hang on, I'm just gonna push you to the top of this first dune so you can see the water.

"Hey, I'm going fishing for a little bit, okay? Make us a nice fish stew for dinner. Wind's not too bad, is it? You'll be okay? Or you want to come with me? No? okay."

I gathered my gear and slung the pack onto its dolly. Behind the dunes, the sand leveled out to hillocks, easier to traverse than the dunes on seaside. The weather was now calm on the inland side, mere ripples. I baited and set out the folding crab traps in thigh-deep water, attached buoys. Left them both near some submerged wood, sunken logs? Parts of old boats? Not sure, but a great hiding place for crabs.

Going up the shore a ways, I shook out the purse net, waded out, grabbed an edge in my teeth and tossed the net in a wide arc. Pulled the cord, drawing the weighted bottom of the net into a pocket, and dragged the whole thing to shore where I examined what's there. A mixture of critters flapped, waved legs and claws, blew bubbles through mouths and gill slits. Pitiful, but yummy. I sorted out the good stuff, tossed back the rest. Repeated until I got tired, which is sooner than it used to be but there we have it.

I sat back against a fallen tree to catch my breath, tasting the savory air, rich as meat. A breeze of terns wafted down on the inland shore for a spot of evening grazing. A gust of laughing gulls, raucous and sudden as jays, scattered the terns for no reason that I could see except they're gulls. Enough. I heaved myself to my feet and loaded the dolly.

I returned with a pretty good haul. In triumph, I showed Honey the harvest: two irate blue crabs, each nearly a foot from shell-tip to shell-tip, a double handful of shrimp, and a bewildered mullet that seems to have zigged when the rest of the school zagged. I fried him up, boiled the crustaceans, and squeezed the juice of a fresh satsuma over the whole thing. Odd, I know, but pretty tasty.

Honey, as usual, didn't have much appetite. After all my coaxing, she showed no interest in the bounty. I fed her broth from her lunchtime soup; most of it dribbled down her chin. I'm not sure how much longer this can continue.

I smacked my lips over the last juicy bit of leg meat from the crab and gave a little chuckle at a memory it jogged.

"Hon, 'member that big argument we had, before we went on the road? You said, 'Patricia, I don't care if Marauders are right down the Three-Mile Track! I want to go find what's out there. I'd rather face untold dangers than have to eat another frog leg!'

'Marguerite,' I told you, 'I will not endanger us both out there just for fancy city food. I won't let you do it, either.' And I didn't, did I? Not then, anyway.

Now here we are, in the outside world like you wanted, and still no fancy city food."

The whole thing just weighed me down right then and I sighed. "Not that you could eat it if we had it,"

I looked over at my love of over fifty years. She gazed silently back at me out of her sunken eyes. I sighed again but that didn't really ease the tightness under my breastbone.

"Honey, I'm so sorry I was such a stubborn fool for so long. Here we are in the wild world you've wanted for so long, and it's too late for you to enjoy any of it, that I can see. I wish we could have one more argument. I said, remember? I said I wished you'd shut up your nagging and give me some peace for a change, and now you've shut up for good."

I brushed away a tear; must have been wind-blown sand. I reached across and adjusted her shawl. "Wind's picking up. Guess we'd better get you inside, huh?"

I wheeled her back up the ramp and settled her near the heater outflow, but not too close. Her skin was so fragile, I hated to think of its getting more dry and papery than it already was. I had replaced her right foot into its pantleg more than once, and I feared it would crumble the next time.

I covered the coals with the now-cool sand and packed up the gear to wash and put away.

An empty beach at sunset is a very romantic place to be, as long as you have your nearest and dearest with you.

GEEZER DYKE

DANNY SETS HER MUG ON the piano bar, drawing a frown from Thomás.

"Oops," she mutters. She leans down to the next table and grabs a cocktail napkin, ignoring the scowl from the napkin's former owner. She raises the mug, slopping beer over the side and plops the napkin, printed with the cartoon of a tortoise wearing a serape, a sombrero, and a tipsy grin and holding up an umbrella drink with 'Señor Tortuga' emblazoned on its side, into the now-spreading puddle.

"Dio," mutters Thomás, "Danny, every night you spill your beer on the exact spot on my piano."

Danny grins, teeth gleaming whitely against her brown face. "Hell, you don't mind. Every night, I make you enough in tips to revarnish this old tank," (she punctuates this with another swipe across the top of the piano with the sopping napkin), "at least once a year."

She turns around, leans back against the piano, takes a long slow breath, and begins to croon, Thomás automatically following her lead. "Meet Me in St. Louis, Louis" is followed by "Chicago", and Danny's voice grows more strong and sure with each song.

"Christ," says the former owner of Danny's napkin, "She sounds just like those old Judy records my damned brother used to play." He's been considering decking the old dyke since she took his napkin without a by-your-leave, not because he cares about the fucking napkin, he thinks the stupid turtle looks like an asshole, but just on general principles. He's realized in time how that would look to his admiring girlfriend.

Danny is indeed an *old* dyke, and a small, weedy-looking one at that. Under her leather tan, the mellow brown of an old bowling-ball bag, lurks the golden tinge of jaundice.

"My liver's shot," she often jokes to her business partner Mako, "It's shot and I don't give a shit." And she laughs hoarsely, sometimes to the point of coughing. Liver notwithstanding, she goes down the road to Señor Tortuga nearly every evening, to exchange an evening of singing for an evening of free (watered, to be sure) beer, wandering home only when the bar closes.

When she'd first moved to this little port town in Mexico, the taxi drivers vied for her patronage at the end of the evening, deeming Danny another wealthy Anglo in a hurry to part with her cash. And Danny, the soul of generosity when in her cups, always fished vaguely in her pockets at the end of the unexpected three-block drive home.

"LEMME GIVE YOU, WAIT, HERE, I gotta little something for ya…" The bemused driver would look at the wads of paper pressed into his hands, pesos, dollar bills, bar napkins, sometimes bearing phone numbers or lipstick prints. If the total take was less than the tourist price, a driver might follow her, protesting, to the door of the shack Danny'd purchased, finding his protest beamingly ignored.

"S'all right, Manolo," Danny would slur, "You're a good guy, keep the change." And the flimsy-looking door would swing shut in his face, the lock clicking firmly into place, and no amount of hammering would avail the driver, whose name might actually be Miguel, Jesus, or Fernando.

Word gets around quickly, however. Danny is no rich tourist seeking a walk on the wild side. The elderly lesbiana is another expatriate retiree. She augments her small pension check by working for Mako, another US expatriate who operates a diving boat business that supports the cruise ships.

It had taken Danny less than a week to pick up her second occupation at Señor Tortuga. She and Mako had stopped by the tavern for "a coupla drinks to set us up" and decided to stay for the remainder of their drinking lives.

"'Member that time, Thomás?" Danny is fond of reminiscing to Thomás' weary nods, "What was it you played that first time, was it 'Over the Rainbow' or 'You Made Me Love You'?"

"Neither, Danny," he always mutters, and Danny continues tossing out the names of every song Garland may have sung, with maybe a few Tony Bennetts thrown in. Truth is, even Thomás isn't sure which song he'd been playing, adrift in that trancelike state where his hands played one piano-bar song after another, his mind wandering over any number of subjects: How many more payments are due on his elegant black performing suit, a snatch of dialog from a movie he watched on television on his day off, what numbers to play on this week's lottery.

Whatever the song was, he'd drifted back to his surroundings, vaguely annoyed by what sounded, at first, like yet another tiresome drunk trying to sing along. Imagine his surprise, indeed, to hear a voice, whiskey-roughened to be sure, but pure and perfectly on key. Not only that but the Americano (an elderly man, was it? No, a woman but obviously a lesbian woman) knew all the words, even to the next verse, and all the ones after it.

Experimentally he'd changed the tempo slightly—and the woman followed, confidently. A subtle key change? Caramba! The woman harmonized! Exquisite! *She* was making *him* sound better! He smiled, nodded encouragement, but the woman seemed not to notice, so enmeshed in the song was she.

Song followed song; if she knew the song (and as long as the music remained pre-'60s and popular, she did), she sang it, and the patrons applauded wildly. If she didn't know the song, she sat silently nodding her head along with the music, sipping her beer. His tips had been enormous that night, even after Thomás had pressed a handful of bills upon her.

"Come in again, Señorita," he'd said politely, even enthusiastically, all unaware that this *gringa* had moved in right on the outskirts of the strip that bisected the harbor town, and would be such an annoying asset to his evening performances.

*

DANNY EASES OUT FROM UNDER the pale dead weight of the arm. She marvels, as she has for years, at how heavy a woman's arm becomes once she is satisfied and drifting off to sleep. She lowers the arm gently onto the mattress and slides out of bed, tugging her boxer shorts back into place.

Nowadays she retains her t-shirt and shorts in bed; years ago she'd had no difficulty baring her body before a woman. Trim, compact, smooth of skin, it hadn't occurred to her or any of her friends to try to protect their bodies from the long-term effects of sun, smoke and alcohol, nor from stripping off their clothes and launching themselves, proudly naked, into bed with their girlfriends.

They'd played softball through the long summer afternoons, sitting in the dugout, laughing, smoking, tossing butts onto the gravel floor and adjourning to Terry's Club (actually owned by the local syndicate; there was no Terry) afterwards. They'd put away one beer after another until the bar closed, perfectly convinced those golden summers would last their lifetimes.

With this anonymous woman asleep in her bed, Danny shakes her head ruefully at the ruin she's become. Smooth bands of muscle are now crepe-wrapped ropes looping down like suspension bridge cables. Her skin is splotched unevenly, islands of freckles now spreading into atolls. Her hair is thinned where it should be thick, yet there are hairs sprouting on skin that should, in Danny's opinion, still be smooth.

It's evident that femmes of a certain age feel the same way, or even more so. This woman, for instance, had let Danny strip off her slacks (What do they call those short pants? Used to be 'pedal-pushers' but Danny thinks it's something different these days) and shiny nylon underpants, but firmly retained her bra and the little skimpy tank top. She doesn't seem to want Danny to touch them at all. Must have *really* saggy tits, Danny decides.

YET, OLD OR NEARLY-OLD, WOMEN are even now willing to come home with her. Danny isn't sure why this is, given that back in the USA, she was just a retired old dyke geezer with a part-time job and, after Ruthie, no self-respecting woman had the slightest interest in her. It's true that when Ruthie had reluctantly packed her things and moved from their shared apartment, Danny'd kind of lost all her starch and vinegar. So how had coming to Mexico changed all that?

"Why'd you move down here, Mako? The climate?"

Raucous laughter. "Naw, the pussy."

"Same here." There *is* something about being an otherwise ordinary, displaced American, doing an ordinary day's work, in this exotic setting that seems to draw women of a certain age. She and Mako gather the day's gaggle of divers of all skill levels, ashore for a day or more from their cruise ships. Mako delivers the standard orientation spiel during the shuttle bus ride to the marina from the port, and Danny gets them all geared up for a one- or two-tank dive, and guides them safely through their reef adventure. By the time Reef Diver, a homely but well-maintained working boat, hauls its cargo of relaxed and often sunburned tourists back to the docks, Danny and Mako know whether this day's group will yield a companion for the evening.

Women who travel in groups with their girlfriends ("girls" being anything from twenty-five to seventy) away from jobs, husbands, and judgmental siblings like to kick up their heels, Danny has found.

This woman (what was her name? Lucinda? Lucille? Celia?), now awake from her nap, begins to pull her pants on reluctantly. This one's a live wire, for certain. Danny can see she's ready to start again. What the hell, you only go around once.

"Hey, let me take this off," Danny tugs at the skimpy green top, "We know each other pretty well by now, huh?"

The woman pulls back, and then relents. "I hope you're not turned off," she says, turning shyly away. She crosses her arms, takes hold of the sides of the shirt and pulls it over her head. She leans forward to allow Danny to unfasten her bra. It slides down her arms.

"No shit," Danny tells Mako later, "I took off her bra and her left tit fell off!" She tries to make a joke of this, but her voice lacks its usual insouciance.

"Left tit? Wow." Mako tries to play along, "Good thing it wasn't the right one, huh?"

"Yeah," Danny seems distracted; the joke falls dead on the dock between them. She shakes her head. "No. Right tit, now I think of it. It was the one on *my* left. She'd had it cut off. Cancer."

"Yeah, well, you know they do that sometimes. Guess if they think you're gonna die they just send you home with all your parts. Kinda like, 'Have a good time in the time ya got left.'"

"Hey, Mako. C'mon. *Cancer.* She's gonna die anyway. They just do that stuff to, you know, drag it out longer."

"Naw, man. Not everybody dies nowadays. Lotsa people survive cancer. That's why they call 'em *survivors*, for crissake. Like they just got home from a shipwreck. Or a war or something."

"Huh. That's just what this gal said."

"I haven't been a survivor for very long," was what the woman had told Danny, "I'm still afraid of what other people will think or feel."

Good thing Danny'd made a life practice of hiding feelings. She made her sincerest grin and dragged the woman back to the bed as if having a tit fall onto the floor was the coolest thing she'd ever seen.

Must have convinced the woman, too, because she'd lingered over dressing afterwards. Danny had heaved an inward sigh of relief when the fake tit had finally disappeared into the lacy bra and been fastened back into place.

"Come on, I'll buy you dinner. Our ship doesn't leave until 7:00 this evening."

With a show of reluctance, Danny shakes her head. "Can't, babe. Mako and I have a full schedule this afternoon. I gotta round up some more blocks of ice and hustle them down to the marina. Hey, it's been wonderful."

The woman shakes her own head, disgusted with herself. Picking up a complete stranger, "rough trade" she thinks it's called. Surprisingly, though, Danny's lovemaking wasn't rough. Her dried and sinewy hands were gentle, knowing, tender, her embrace warm. She sincerely didn't seem to mind the prosthesis or the discolored, scarred surface where the real thing had been.

Danny's eyes even now, in her hurry to finish her working day, look into the woman's in a kindly way. The woman picks up the monogrammed carry bag that holds her still-damp swimsuit. The initials "C.A." gleam in still-new brass.

Ah, that's the name. "Celia, I mean it, sincerely, if you're ever down this way, come diving with us again. I'll have Mako take us out to a special reef we know, a place where we never take the tourists; we'll explore it together."

Celia's heart gives a little hop and then steadies. She takes a breath, steps back avoiding Danny's hug. "I'll do that. You take care of yourself, you hear?" She lets herself out, closing the door firmly behind her. In the blinding lemon-peel sun, she waves down a taxi for the half-mile trip back to the cruise docks; she could have walked but she's disoriented.

*

DANNY DUMPS THE FINAL 40-POUND ice block into Reef Diver's built-in cooler and begins to feed drinks (Pepsi, Diet Sprite, Corona Long-Necks, Ice Mountain water in sealed 'Please recycle' bottles) into its thirsty mouth. "Hey, Mako. You ever been in love? I mean really in love?"

Mako grunts as he hoists a double tank over the side. His goddamn back is giving him fits again; he welcomes the opportunity to sit down and rest it, looking thoughtful.

"I been married once, is that what you mean?"

"Married because you wanted to be together for life, you mean?"

"Yeah, I guess so. It's been a while. Got two kids, too. Grown, of course. I get cards sometimes, but they don't come to visit. You know."

"Busy lives, yeah."

"Yeah. You ever been serious about anyone? He chuckles. 'Husband, or anything?'" He pretends to duck as Danny cocks an arm and feints a throw at his head with a Coke can. It makes him wince and he straightens quickly. She smiles, reaches the can down into the cooler. She keeps her back turned to Mako as she works, keeping her voice casual.

"Lived with this woman for nearly twenty years."

"What happened? She get tired of your ugly face?"

"Kind of. You know, I hardly drank at all that whole time? I quit the smoking, too, it was grossing my girlfriend out."

"That's rich. Quit smoking and then sing all night in the smog bank at Tortuga. Twenty years without drinking, though, man. Did you do that AA thing?"

"Naw. Well, I tried that once; that was before Ruthie, though. Made me feel like an asshole, saying that stuff. Everyone talking about their 'higher powers' like a bunch of Christers but without the hymn-singing."

"So, how'd you quit for twenty years?"

"I didn't mean to. When we first got together I just, you know, didn't need to get wasted every night."

Mako grins. "Yeah, I remember how that was. You have better things to do every night."

"Yeah." They both sit there grinning like a pair of possums on a moonlit evening.

Danny isn't sure why she's thinking so much about Ruthie. She thinks, though, it might be because of Celia's eyes. Damn, now that she thinks of it, they're just like Ruthie's, before the cancer.

Danny hadn't really been interested in the woman though of course she'd noticed Celia's furtive glances. The red hair was okay, sort of coppery with blondie lights when the sun reflected off it, but then she had that freckly pale redhead skin that goes blotchy red in the sun unless, like Celia has done, it's slathered thickly with high-octane suntan lotion that's supposed to smell like pineapple or coconut or something. Fish-belly white, Danny calls it in her own mind, but as the day wears on the pale skin doesn't seem quite such an issue. The woman's eyes are brown, a dark velvet brown that contrasts starkly with her copper-gold hair and that freckle-banana skin.

Ruthie's hair wasn't red; it was light brown with goldish lights, like the hull of a live-oak acorn. Her skin wasn't darkly tanned like Danny's had always been, but a creamy white that glowed softly in the streetlight that filtered through the curtains at night. Ruthie's eyes were dark brown, almost black, like smudges of charcoal on a sheet of vellum. Looking into those eyes made Danny feel dizzy. The sadness in Celia's dark eyes yesterday afternoon, masked with dignity as she let herself out....

"... Danny, I'm not really leaving you. You've already left me." By that time the chemo had thinned Ruthie's hair and her skin had gone paper white.

"The whole group waited, Danny. I was so embarrassed; what could I say?"

Danny had sucked in breath, tried to stay back where Ruthie couldn't smell the booze. Which, of course, had permeated the entire living room, small as it was. "I'm sorry, babe, I just lost track of the time."

Ruthie rarely lost her temper. With difficulty, she'd held it in then.

"I know this is hard for you too, Danny. But you know what? When your mom died of cancer, it was thirty years ago. A lot more people died of cancer back then. Every day there are new treatments...."

Danny hates that word, "treatments". A treat is something delicious, fun, jolly. What Ruthie was choosing to face was poison, radiation, mutilation, and she'd wanted Danny to be part of her "support system" as she endured it. And at the end of it all, it would be Danny, not some bunch of assholes from her goddamn "support system" who would sit beside Ruthie's deathbed and help usher her out of their life together.

Danny'd gritted her teeth, looked away, and muttered again that she was sorry, she just forgot. Ruthie had shaken her head, and in the next few weeks the slow torturous separation expanded until Ruthie, like Celia, had sadly but firmly pulled the door closed behind her. That final click of the door latch.

Danny was pretty deeply in the bag by then, enough so that instead of throwing her head back and baying her grief at the moon like a demented coyote, she'd just muttered "Bitch," and used her pocketknife to slit the seal on a new fifth.

SHE NEVER SAW RUTHIE AGAIN, though she knew Ruthie had been by the apartment several times in her absence. Instead of being forced to watch Ruthie erode away with the disease and the "treatments", Danny had chosen to find Ruthie's presence eroding away behind her back. Ruthie's possessions and accretions slipped out of the apartment in increments: the sewing kit Ruthie used to hem Danny's new jeans (always an inch too long, for some reason), the hallway mirror where Ruthie used to check to see that her skirt hung perfectly straight, the wok that they had used about three times a year.

By the time Danny had packed her own clothes and headed south to start a new life, all that remained were empty bottles and the gifts Danny had given to her dearest, back when they were both healthy and happy.

Mako sits silently, fingering a rough place on the gunwale, his own private thoughts occupying him. Danny's grateful for that, sure that her own pain and guilt are obvious as she remembers. Mako feels her eyes now turned to him, recollects the thread of the conversation.

"So, after the thrill was gone, you started drinking again, right? And she finally got fed up and walked out?" Danny now sees that's where Mako's own marriage went.

"Yeah, sort of." Then idly, "You ever think about looking your wife up again?"

"Naw, she'd hate living in Mexico. She never liked the diving, either. You?"

"I think she's dead. Maybe. I mean, yeah. Gotta be."

"Shit. Bummer." Danny can see him considering whether to inquire and forestalls him. "Yeah, cancer. Last time I saw her, she probably had about three months to live."

"Bummer," he says again, and they're both saved by the arrival of Armand, the tour organizer. He collects Mako for the drive to the cruise port in the shuttle van.

"Welcome aboard," Danny greets this new band of excited tourists. Most of them think she's a small, weather-beaten man, and the rest don't really care.

*

"HEY, MAN, THERE'S NO WAY I can do that. Can't you reschedule?"

Mako, who feels like a shark has taken a bite out of his shoulder blade, would like to punch Danny. Since he needs her as much as she needs him, he takes a slow breath and tries to shift to a more comfortable position.

"It's easy, Danny. You've helped me with all that shit dozens of times. Armand will do the driving, you get all the names on the checklist, take the damned tickets, give the spiel on the way over here, and by then I'll be here to pilot us out."

"Yeah, it's easy. Easy for you. It's that (she drops her voice into a jocular boom that eerily resembles Mako's bass) 'Welcome to Reef Diver Tours!' crap that I'd just as soon skip. It sounds good when you do it; I'll sound like an asshole."

"You'll sound like a bigger asshole if I have to wring your scrawny neck, dammit." Wincing, he gets up and limps to his aging Jeep, hauls himself into it, and with a clash of gears, punctuated with "Owwww, shit!" he drives away. He's going to the pharmacy to refill his Percodan prescription, something he should have done two weeks ago but didn't want to spend his beer money on it.

"Damn!" says Danny and repeats it more vehemently as Armand pulls up in the cruise shuttle van. She grabs the clipboard Mako has left for her, and scrabbles among the detritus on the footlocker until she finds a pen that works.

She doesn't mind the collecting of tickets, always putting them carefully into the pocket of her outer wrap, mindful of the day Mako forgot and shoved them into the back pocket of his swim trunks and, fuming, had to peel them carefully, one at a time, away from the sodden mess ("If we don't turn them in, we don't get paid"). Doesn't mind collecting names on the check-in sheet ("Sorry, I can't make out the name. Snxt?" "No, Smith."), because if they don't turn in the same number of tourists they left with, "Well, you get the picture," Mako says. Danny thinks of them as library books that must be returned in time or there's a fine. A really big fine.

She stands outside the shuttle bus now, feeling like a dork as she holds up the sign that says "Reef Diver Scuba Tours" on a broken-off piece of yardstick. She watches folks come off the ship, showing their ship passes and passports to the inspectors at the gate and then looking around stupidly at the mass of violently colored buses, taxis, shuttle vans, their guides calling out the names of the tours like carnival barkers. Danny keeps her trap shut for the most part unless one of "their" tourists shows up and needs to be checked in (take the ticket, ask them politely to sign the sheet, assure them the bus will indeed leave on time and will get them back on time) or unless a stray looks directly at the sign and asks, "Is this the shuttle for the Museum Tours?"

Mostly, her mind is racing, trying to remember the main points of Mako's orientation speech. It brings back the sweaty-palmed memory of seventh-grade speech class where you had to make an informative speech, an entertaining speech, a persuasive speech. Some of the kids (the "A" students and a few boys whom she now realizes were gay and would eventually go on to theater companies) actually enjoyed the class, brought "visual aids" and had to be told to cut their speeches short.

Danny, who enjoyed only math and science, neither of which led to a possible career for a girl back then, stumbled through the assignments, accepted her generously-awarded "C" and tried never again to be in that position. Somehow, singing in front of an audience was different— she sang for herself and for the song, and, drunk or sober, rarely noticed if there were folks hearing or even in the room.

"Welcome aboard, ladies and gentlemen. While we're riding to the marina where we'll, uh...." she subvocalizes. "What? Sorry. No, this is the two-tank scuba tour. The shopping bus is two down that way. *That way*. Yes. You have a nice day now."

Mako has to remind her now and then, that these folks are on vacation, they don't expect to have to think for themselves, and they're in a new place and disoriented. Danny started to point out, the first time he said this, that they can't be any more disoriented than she was when she first stepped down from the rattletrap bus in the town square, alone and with no plans beyond what she'd found in an article in a retirement magazine.

The difference is, she now realizes, that she was running away from Ruthie's death, and ready to seriously begin seeking her own, so it was no big deal if things worked out, if she had a good time or even made it through the first week. The folks who wander bemusedly down the gangway from the cruise ships are seeking life, not death. They want treats, not treatments, and aren't paying large sums of their hard-earned money for Danny to make judgments about them.

Danny takes another ticket and offers the clipboard to a young, awesomely fit man (college student, probably) in baggy trunks emblazoned with red and orange flowers. Her eyes wander vaguely over the groups of people passing by as he scribbles his particulars onto the page; she freezes.

Three women have just passed by. The one in the middle has a head of short curls, a little thin but still brown with gold lights glinting in the blinding sun, just the color of live-oak acorns. Possibly, the woman in the middle could have dark brown, almost black eyes, just like smudges of charcoal.

Danny tries to speak, coughs, and then says, too loudly, "Excuse me?" The women turn, casually curious, eyebrows raised. Nope. They're that green that's sort of muddy in the wrong light.

"Sorry. Thought you were someone I used to know."

The woman smiles briefly and the three of them turn away.

＊

THAT NIGHT AT SEÑOR TORTUGA, Danny is absent-minded, lacking her usual mellow fire. Thomás frowns. If Danny doesn't sound good he's on his own here. Not that he won't be fine on his own. But still.

"You okay, Danny? Not getting sick are you?"

"Naw, just old. Old and stupid," she says, and gives more of her attention to "Memories". She hates this song, but the patrons eat it up.

Encouraged, Thomás eases into "If You Go Away," a favorite for both of them. Tricky range, gotta keep from bottoming out on the "when the night bird sang" part. Audiences always got a little misty-eyed at this song and often tipped big at the end.

The voice rises, smooth with a touch of added richness, "… but if you stay, I'll give you a day like no day has been, or will be again—"

Astoundingly, the voice cracks. Danny turns, grabs for her beer mug. Her face twitches and she slams the mug back down onto the piano top.

"Ay!" yells Thomás, but Danny ignores him. She turns and stiff-arms her way out the door. She doesn't return for the rest of that night. Thomás finishes up his shift on his own, as he used to do.

He hopes she'll come back tomorrow. Or the next day. Why wouldn't she? But it worries him.

A port stop during a cruise disembarked us in Mexico, facing a row of tour vans and buses. Most of these were staffed by sign-wielding native folks with weary, worldly-wise faces; obviously they did this job for the living it provided and not because they found it fun. One of the tour guides was a lesbian, white, aging none too gracefully, and it was evident from her accent that she'd begun life as a North American Midwesterner. She looked and clearly felt, however, more akin to her brown-skinned career associates than to the flocks of North American tourists who surrounded her. We wondered what, or who, had led her to this path. And of course, romantics that we are, we wondered whom she went home to when her day of tourist-wrangling was over.

IT'S A RULE

STEEN GRIMACED AND SHIFTED HER backpack; some essential object poked into her back, right in that tricky place over the point of her right shoulder blade. "You're so thin," people often said in that envious way, but sometimes Steen wished she possessed the genes for a little more padding. Lots of butches were round, and they didn't wince whenever they sat or leaned against hard surfaces.

Irritably she watched Pattye study the self-check-in monitor. Airport noises buzzed and babbled around her. "C'mon, c'mon," she thought, but did not say, "You've done this dozens of times and every time you act like you never saw a touch screen before. Are you really stupid, or what?" She plopped her backpack onto the floor, assumed a look of strained patience, and waited.

Pattye read the screen again, trying to make sense of the question. Did her backpack count as a piece of carry-on luggage? Did her fanny pack? What about the baggie of corn chips that dangled from her hand? For nearly ten years she and Steen had checked in at airports together. "Before the Fall," as they called the pre-9/11 travel days, they'd stood at a counter where a human joked with them about inconsequential things while they filled out the little cardboard address tags on elastic strings, affixed them to suitcase handles, wrestled the suitcases onto the low shelf, no questions asked.

In the later days of self-check-in there had been less joking, less, well, freedom in the act of escaping daily life and flying off into the wide-open skies. Pattye studied the screen prompts. Damn! "How can anyone concentrate," she thought, but did not say, "with you glowering over there like Old Stone-Face?"

Steen, fed up with waiting for her soon-to-be-ex-partner, did a smart right-about-face. She nearly went sprawling over the backpack she'd set down a moment before. Pain shot up the outside of her ankle. "Owww! Shit, sonofabitch!" Dragging the backpack by a strap, she hobbled over to the shiny and generally uncomfortable backless bench by the wall and fell onto it. She nursed her ankle and her resentment toward Pattye. She knew she was being unfair; she'd just forgotten the backpack was right beside her, and knowing she was being unreasonable only made her angrier.

A fleeting expression of concern flickered across Pattye's face; she clamped it down immediately and thought, "Serves you right, old crab. If you weren't so busy trying to make me hurry, you wouldn't have tripped." She knew she was being a bitch. She didn't care.

It didn't seem so very long ago that, had one of them stumbled, the other would have dropped everything and rushed to the rescue. "Are you okay, dearest?" "Sweetheart! Let me get that for you!" "Here, sweetie, sit down and I'll go find some ice."

The first time Steen, whose ankles seemed to be her weakness, had stumbled into a hole on the softball field and laid herself up for nearly a week, Pattye had told her severely, "Don't fall in any more holes! It's a rule!"

"It's a rule," Steen had agreed, and was more careful of holes in the ground thereafter.

No, not so very long ago at all, and now here they were, stuck together like rabid Siamese twins ("conjoined twins", Pattye's mind hastily corrected), hating every instant of proximity. Well, but not much longer. They'd make this final trip to North Carolina, close up the house, dispose of all the clutter they'd accumulated over the years, and put the house on the market.

Unlike the overpriced condominium monstrosities that lined the barrier islands, modest houses further inland were in demand. Retirees wanted to live in this moderate climate, and Pelicans, their own little vacation paradise, was just the right size for a very new or very old couple. Indeed, it had been their own dream to grow old in the bungalow together.

Pattye now sat on the ubiquitous hard airport bench after the security unpleasantness, struggling back into her walking shoes. She looked up in time to see Steen, face drawn with unhappiness and pain, scrambling to collect her belongings from the bins on the conveyer belt. Pattye felt a melting instant of tenderness, or maybe it was just old habit making itself felt.

Steen caught her looking, frowned, and limped to a different bench far from Pattye's, her pack dangling like something dead from one hand, her shoes in the other.

Silently, separately, they arrived at their gate. Pattye wandered the waiting area, scrounging discarded sections of *USA Today*.

Why the hell do you have to collect other people's cruddy old papers like some wino? Steen thought but did not say. It's not as if they couldn't afford to buy a fresh clean newspaper once in a while. She pulled out her paperback, Amy Tan's latest, and immersed herself in it until the call for them to board.

Their seats were in the last row, what Steen used to call "the ha-ha row" because the airline's joke was on the hapless souls who first realized that the row in front of them could tilt their seats back but the last row persons could only sit bolt upright with seat backs practically in their laps.

Since Steen and Pattye barely spoke except for the merest essentials, Pattye hadn't realized that Steen had failed to do the on-line check-in this time. Steen, in a fit of spite, hadn't bothered. "Let Pattye do it for a change", had been her thought, a bit of cut-off-your-nose bitchery she now regretted.

Silently they prepared to cram into their claustrophobic stalls.

"Why didn't we try to get seats in different rows?" Pattye wondered, though not aloud, as she wrestled her backpack into the overhead bin. Steen, taller by six inches, used to help her with this.

Steen, meanwhile, was cramming her backpack under the seat before her and wondering, "Why didn't we take separate flights?"

She couldn't help recalling their first flight together, when the agent had asked them if they were travelling together.

"A simple 'yes' would have sufficed," she'd told Pattye as they walked down the jet way, *"You didn't need to tell her all our personal business."*

Pattye stopped in her tracks, causing a grumbling traffic jam behind them, and stared at Steen. "What, you didn't want her to know this was our first vacation together as lovers? Whyever not?"

Steen took her arm and started her walking again. "Well, there's no reason for strangers to know every little detail."

"Oh, stop with that. You know and I know that when people say 'My personal life is nobody else's business', they're really just saying, 'I'm a self-loathing homosexual and I'm afraid people won't like me if they know who I really am'."

The woman behind them chuckled audibly, causing Steen to blush, and chimed in, "I agree with your girlfriend. Why shouldn't strangers know you're a couple?"

"Okay, okay," Steen mumbled, "I get the point."

"No closets in our house unless they're for the clothes, right?" demanded Pattye. "It's a rule."

"Okay, it's a rule."

"Atta girl," said the woman behind them.

A three-hour, interminable, flight in close proximity. Not so very long ago, the moveable arm rest would have been raised so their bodies fit companionably together. Steen's shoulders were already feeling tight, not from the heavy backpack but from the strain of leaning away from Pattye.

Years ago, like all lovers, they'd had their first fight. Neither one could have dredged up what actually started it, though possibly it just boiled down to low blood sugar and too many obligations crammed into too little time. But they both remembered what Steen had said that evening.

"We have to make up before we go to bed, Pattye."

"No! I'm still mad at you!"

"Hey, I'm pretty pissed at you, too. But we have to stay up and figure this thing out, or you know what will happen?"

Sullenly, "What?"

"We'll go to sleep in the same bed, but there'll be this little cellophane wall between us. And if we don't tear it down soon, it'll stay there and next time we fight it'll get a little thicker and harder to tear down. And pretty soon it will turn into cardboard, and then plywood, and before we know it there'll be this big thick brick wall between us and that'll be the end of our loving each other."

Hearing this made Pattye cry. And so of course they had cried together then, and made up and gone to bed holding each other as though they feared some ogre would pull them apart.

"No cellophane walls," they agreed soberly, "It's a rule."

The plane's headlong rush down the runway failed to terrify Pattye as it usually did. "I don't give a damn if we do crash right now," she thought.

Steen did not reach comfortingly for Pattye 's hand. "Serves her right if she's terrified," she thought, and rustled her in-flight magazine instead of saying that. Pattye, annoyed, affected not to notice.

It was odd, their breakup. There had been no catalyst, no affair or grand betrayal, no alcoholism or problem children to drive the wedge. They had done it themselves, almost absent-mindedly.

Neither could have told you, really, when the lingering morning kisses metamorphosed into perfunctory absent-minded pecks and finally disappeared altogether. Nor how it was that one morning Pattye found herself across the breakfast bar from Steen, watching with distaste as Steen, elbows braced apart and a paperback in one fist, shoveled Fruit-Loops into her mouth. Steen would chew each mouthful twice, mouth decently closed, and then give a little audible "smek!" before really powering up to noisy mastication. Then she'd gulp the resulting mush hastily before delivering another spoonful. Pattye began to sit elsewhere at breakfast.

Nor could Steen have told you when she first noticed how often Pattye punctuated her sentences with "Like I said", whether she'd ever spoken that particular idea before or not, nor why Steen didn't just say, "Pattye, would you knock that off? It's annoying."

Pattye began sitting up late watching television and falling asleep on the couch because they had made a rule that no television or computer was allowed in the sanctity of their bedroom. Steen went to the ball game with her childhood friend and best pal Nicky without bothering to call home. Pattye, weeping, had flown at Steen when she returned home. "I thought something had happened to you!" she wailed. Steen had promised never to make that mistake again, and kept her promise.

Pattye though, on the evening of receiving the coveted Lead Analyst position at her office, had gone out with the team for drinks afterwards and in the rush of euphoria and good feeling, had forgotten to invite Steen along or even call home at all.

Although Steen still kept her promise to always call, she dawdled just a little longer on the daily drive home from work. Pattye worked longer hours, and when Steen grumbled, pointed out that her salary enabled them to pay off their dream retirement home ahead of time.

Charming quirks stopped being so charming. Their teeth-gritting silent endurance became the final mortar in the ever-thickening wall.

Last year had been the last nearly happy trip they'd taken to Pelicans. Pelicans was an older two-bedroom cottage near the intra-coastal waterway. The house was built for ordinary non-tourist people to live in. It had rag rugs scattered on scarred hardwood floors and a plain white stove with a chip in the enamel, dabbed with Rustoleum to halt corrosion from the damp ocean air.

Pattye and Steen together would load the car for the 10-hour drive to the coast, or look up discounted airline tickets and car rentals. The two of them always dropped off their luggage at the house and then went to the grocery together to stock up on the week's groceries.

Pattye, ever practical, had first suggested that one of them stay at Pelicans to 'open the house', turning on the refrigerator and the water heater, making up the beds, while the other went for the groceries.

Laughing, they'd agreed that saving time wasn't the point of their trip to Pelicans, that enjoying the time together was. "It's a rule", they'd agreed.

Last year, though, Pattye had gone for the groceries while Steen wiped out the sinks, plugged in the refrigerator, and made sure the toilet flushed and didn't leak. Any weeping that was done during that bittersweet last week at Pelicans was done alone.

Now most of the weeping and stormy exchanges were done. All that remained was cold ashes, sadness, and this trip to Pelicans for the division and disposal of "property", that arid and dispassionate word for the treasures they'd garnered during times of happiness. Side by side, silently, not touching, they felt the plane lift upwards and begin its turn towards the east coast.

Pattye rustled her paper. Steen brooded over her magazine.

It happened fast, as things do when you are inside a pressurized metal tube hurtling through the air at hundreds of miles an hour with nowhere to go but down. There was a surprisingly low-key "plunk," followed by several grumbling, garbage-disposal noises, and then the airplane gave a nauseating lurch to one side. As it began to straighten out again, the engine noise was strangely lopsided, as though one engine was working madly and the other one lagged.

After an instant's muteness in the entire passenger list, a gabbling broke out. "What is it?" "What's happening?" "Mommy, is the airplane broken?" "Oh, shit."

Steen craned her neck forward, seeking the comforting sight of an attendant. No dice. The one(s) way up front (One? Or two attendants up front? She couldn't remember) were hidden behind a bulkhead. She unbuckled her seat belt and stood up to peer around the bulkhead behind her. The uniformed woman sat, bolt upright, pale but otherwise composed. Except, that was, for the fact that she was speaking quietly but urgently to nobody that Steen could see. Praying? Hallucinating?

"Just our luck," thought Steen, "Plane's gonna crash and we have a religious nut here to help us arrive at our destination." It was only when the woman looked up at Steen in annoyance, waving her back into her seat, that Steen noticed the headset.

"She's talking to the pilot or something," Steen whispered to Pattye. Pattye nodded, numbly. Her eyes filled as she looked, for the first time in weeks, directly into Steen's eyes.

Pattye was green with terror; what she had been expecting every time an airplane took off with her on it had finally come to pass. They were about to die. She would have a minute or two left to breathe, feel her heart pound, speak. Then some sort of frightful agony before the final oblivion. She would never kneel on the earth again, digging in her garden. Never raise a glass of wine with her work mates.

Damn. She would never hold Steen again.

The same falling or burning or ripping asunder would happen to Steen, whom she no longer loved. Bullshit. She raised the arm rest, turned to Steen.

The intercom announcement interrupted them. It came, to Pattye's annoyance, in that rushed "twitter-speak" form of English that so often masqueraded as business courtesy. "Thankavanisday", in place of "Thank you, have a nice day", had been Pattye's former pet peeve. Now she found a new one, in this near-death experience, of being told via intercom, to "Plis remain sted widyer seablts fastn your teatables n seats n upright positions".

She knew the drill as well as any adult airline traveler, but why wouldn't the stupid woman give the passengers any useful information? She could see Steen's frustration also. Assuming the worst, they spoke together, "Steen, we've just *wasted* the entire last year of our lives!", "What the hell have we been doing?"

Again, the metallic crackling voice came over the intercom. Pattye could see Steens's attention wandering from herself and for once did not take it personally. Her own antennae quivered in an attempt to grasp what, if anything, their future held.

"Ladies and gentlemen," began the announcement...

"Thank the goddess", whispered Steen, "This one speaks English." Pattye smiled.

"... the captain has advised me that we have developed a problem with one of the engines and will be returning to the airport immediately. Please remove the safety information card from the seat pocket in front of you and follow along as we prepare the cabin for a possible emergency landing...."

Pattye plucked the bright yellow card from its place. They bent their heads over it. Steen reached with her free hand, to take Pattye's. They tried to focus on the instructions, which included the usual drill of, "Store all loose items under the seat in front of you," and then, "Fasten your seat belt low and tight across your lap."

One of the attendants, an older woman with, Steen noticed, excellent posture, stepped briskly down the aisle, helping the slower passengers to close lap trays and stow loose objects, tweaking and adjusting the cabin and its passengers into some sort of emergency perfection.

"You're losing that newspaper," Steen murmured.

Pattye glanced down to the Living section that was sliding to the floor. "Oh, screw the newspaper".

In front of them, a man spoke softly into his illegally active cell phone. He was weeping. "Mom? I'm so sorry, Mom. I didn't mean any of those things I said. Mom? I love you." He hung up and sobbed quietly.

Pattye reached over and squeezed Steen's hand. "Don't you want to call Nicky and tell her goodbye?"

"Oh, screw Nicky. That time I didn't call you? I didn't forget. Nicky'd been riding my ass about how you always call the shots, and I didn't want her to think I was, you know, pussy-whipped."

"Oh. Screw Nicky."

Steen laughed softly and tuned back to the instructions about how to brace for impact. Impact, for chrissake. Like a wisdom tooth. She and Pattye were wisdom teeth in the mouth of the universe. She realized that she was giddy with terror, oddly enough mixed with a surge of joy. Joy? She and Pattye, together again. She sighed tremulously.

The left engine coughed and made a clattery rumbling sound, like a lawnmower that won't start, but then fell silent again. The passengers, in unison, let out breaths. A child whimpered. Pattye thought it was a child, anyway.

The older attendant cruised briskly but smoothly back up the aisle and disappeared behind the rear bulkhead. Over the susurration of passenger whispers and whimpers, Pattye heard the sharp "Snik!" as the attendant fastened her own seat belt.

None too soon, it seemed. The intercom voice was steady, but intense as it instructed, "Brace, brace, keep your head down until the plane stops, stay down, stay down..."

Steen leaned out into the aisle to squint at the opposite window.

"Down! Keep your heads down," barked the older attendant. Steen leaned back in and obediently ducked her head between her braced arms. She then sneaked a peek at Pattye, who peered interestedly out the window. Gently, Steen reached over and guided Pattye's head around and down. Her hand lingered on the nape of Pattye's neck, feeling the soft skin and tender wisps of curling hair. How fragile that nape appeared! How often she'd nibbled that neck, those little wisps of hair tickling her nose and lips!

"Pattye? Let's not die alone. Let's be together again, just for these last seconds."

"Let's. Hey, maybe we won't die. What about that? Remember that Hudson River thing? Maybe we have another Sully up front there."

"Maybe so. If that's so, when we get to Pelicans we're going to have the best damned vacation anybody ever had. I'll pick up all the sections of newspaper lying around the airport, and you can read 'em all in bed tomorrow morning and I won't gripe a bit."

"And I'll get you a box of Fruit Loops and stay at the table while you snarfle them all down."

"Do I snarfle?"

"Yeah. But it's kinda cute, like that bloodhound in the dog food commercial."

"Thanks." The plane bounced hard; muffled screams erupted around them. Were they on a runway? No, Steen thought, it was just a lurch.

When Steen spent childhood summers at her grandparents' lake house, one of her solitary games was to carefully float an empty clam shell on the calm water and then gradually drip wet sand into it until critical mass was reached and the shell would sink. As it sank, it wallowed from side to side. The next motion the plane made resembled that first sideways wallow. The man in front of them wept on, hopelessly.

"I have an idea." Steen unbuckled her seat belt with shaking hands and managed to thread it through Pattye's belt, then quickly buckled it again.

"So, we'll stay together. No matter what. I promise."

"Together. No matter what. It's a rule."

Pattye linked her arm through Steen's and thus joined, they braced against the seat backs and lowered their heads again.

"It's a rule."

And they kept their promise, for the rest of their lives.

This is a cautionary tale to all long-term couples. The rule is, never *take one another for granted. This could be your last day together.*

NIGHT MANEUVERS AT
THE SEVENTH HOLE

"WHAT THE HELL, ELVIN. YOU know you ain't ever goin huntin again, so you might just as well sell me that old deer rifle now."

"Now wait, Roland you ain't givin me a chance to show you…"

"Or give it to me, you might's well. Maybe I'll give you a nice haunch of venison next time I take it jacking." Roland was joking; he would never hunt out of season.

"Wait a damn minute! What I been tryin to tell you!"

Elvin age 57, was edging up to 400 pounds and was unable to walk more than 50 feet without wheezing like an ancient jackass at the end of the trail, and like as not he'd have to plop down onto the nearest sturdy couch or chair at the end of that. Either way he'd be panting noisily like the old hound dog that he was, leaning forward, hands on wide-spread knees.

He still wasn't sure how that had come about. He'd been a big boy, it was true, but not a fat one. His Momma had seen to that.

"Oh, I know, when a boy gets fat they don't call him fat like they do a girl; they call him 'husky' or 'beefy' like he's a prime steer. Not my boy, no ma'am and no sir."

This came after Elvin had asked to go to McDonald's for lunch with Roland.

And Momma wasn't finished. "No boy of mine is ever gonna end up like some of my patients, big fat men as young as me, stuck in a wheelchair for the rest of their days, legs gone below the knee because of the sugar diabetes." Momma worked at the nursing home down on Davidson Avenue, second shift. Because she wasn't there most of the afternoon, Elvin got to do most of the heavy work in her precious vegetable garden after school. He hated the work and hated the vegetables, but, well, that was Momma. It was just her way.

When Roland's daddy offered to take Elvin along with his own boy hunting, Momma let him go along. "Good protein in venison, and we can always use a wild turkey if you can get one. Don't bring home any raccoons, nasty greasy things."

Elvin wasn't fat as a young man, either. When he married his Dot, she saw to that just as Momma had. Dot had her own garden, like Momma's only she added zucchini, which Elvin found slimier than okra but ate it because, well, Dot. She too liked him to bring home a deer every season and birds for Sunday dinner.

Elvin had stayed "good" for some time after Dot lost her long fight with colon cancer. Before she went, she got in some final directives. "Don't you go eating all those heavy widows casseroles women are gonna bring over after I'm gone." He didn't tell her that now she was in the hospice, they were already bringing over casseroles. Also pies, cakes, and sweet rolls. He brought most of these into the hospice for the nurses, hoping this would bring Dot special treatment.

Much good did any of it do her, he'd thought bitterly over his boneless chicken breast and broccoli. Or him, for that matter. This stuff had no taste, just like his life.

Hell with it. It felt, at first, like cheating on her when he frolicked with takeout from the Shrimp Basket and rib dinners from Sonny's BBQ, but soon he warmed up to the project of packing in as many carbs and grease bombs as would fit in a given evening. Then he got serious about his infidelities and commenced a serious affair with Baskin Robbins.

When Dot looked over his shoulder and shook her head sadly, he set his jaw and stared at the Fishing Channel over his dripping spoon.

When Momma said, "Boy, what did I tell you about getting fat?" he did something he would not have dared to do when she was alive: he sassed her back. "Hush up, Momma. I'm a grown man now." Momma didn't smack him upside the head, only said under her breath, "I don't know about that."

It was some while later that Budweiser edged out his regular paramours, and much later after that when he started telling himself he was fine, just fine as frog's hair, as he slid behind the wheel of his van after a six-pack of longnecks. His sky-blue Econoline van collected mysterious dings and dents that he filled in and finally painted the entire vehicle with primer and called it good. Dot and Momma had less and less to say to him after a year of that.

It was obvious to anyone, not only his boyhood pal Roland, that Elvin's days of taking a rifle into the palmetto scrub in search of animals to shoot were about seventy-five pounds in the past.

Nonetheless, on this day Roland's goading pushed him to his limit. He heaved himself to his feet.

"Now Elvin, you better be careful...." (Roland pronounced that last word as "keerful"). Elvin wheezed and tottered down the uneven path across his back yard.

"Shut up," puffed Elvin as he undid the hasp on the door of his shed and pulled the doors open. His bulk swayed from side to side, but he made it inside and to the seat of a wheeled conveyance, and flopped sideways onto it. The seat gave a low farting "phoosh!" as Elvin's weight imploded its wide plastic cushion.

"What in the *hail* is that?"

"It's why I'm going huntin' again this year. Cost me a job lot, but it's worth it."

The vehicle filled half the shed. It appeared to be a golf cart, but what a golf cart! The normal small wide rubber tires, designed to trundle smoothly over fragile turf, had been exchanged for deep-treaded balloon off-road ones. The usually bright upholstery and roof canopy were camouflage instead. A small winch protruded from the rear of the bastard vehicle, and assorted folded pipes and gizmos littered the rear hatch along with folded tarps, gun rack, and a cooler.

"Extra-duty shocks and ATV tires," Elvin pointed out happily from his perch in the cart. "I can put my rifles right here—" (He indicated the rack with a grandiose sweep of his arm, whacking his wrist a good one. He hardly noticed.) "—and when I reach my stand, I just drop these here side curtains."

He dropped a curtain and peered at Roland through the wide viewing slit. Roland thought he looked like a manic, oversized ferret squinting through the aperture, but forbore to comment.

The curtain snapped back up like a window shade, and Elvin released a catch and pivoted his seat until it faced the rear.

"When I get my deer, I set up this tripod contraption—" He opened a folding tripod and, with the help of a battery-powered gadget, extended the legs; it became a derrick nearly ten feet tall "—and run the cable over it from this winch, and just hoist 'er up!"

Roland shook his head in reluctant admiration but was still dubious. "After you gut 'er out, where do you put the carcass? You ain't got no room on the passenger seat for it to ride in." He chuckled at his own wit, picturing the gutted deer riding grandly and silently along on the bench seat next to Elvin in his balloon-tired vehicle.

Elvin leaned over, still puffing, and unfolded a lever from the floor. He pushed this away from him. A shelf slid out of the floor in the back, large enough, but just barely, to accommodate the body of a full-grown deer.

"Then I just drop 'er onto this, strap 'er on, and head back to my van."

"You ain't got a ramp to drive that thing up in your van," countered Roland. He didn't know why he was raising all these objections to dampen Elvin's joy in his new toy. He didn't know if it was worry or jealousy. Or both.

"Don't need it." Elvin was smug. "My wheelchair lift'll do 'er just fine. Crank the whole thing up and push 'er into the back of the van. She rolls just easy, and just clears the roof. Shut the door and nobody's the wiser."

"You ain't huntin' out of season? Naw, man, tell me you're not that stupid. You'll stand out a mile in that rig."

"Huh-uh. Look at it! Camo, man, and the whole shebang's electric drive. Silent. I'm going out tomorrow night."

"Stupid, man." Then Roland's curiosity got the better of him. "Where?"

"Grace Woods." Elvin's eyes danced.

"You crazy! Man, right next to that big ol golf club?"

"Yup."

"Naw, man. Naw...."

"You come over day after tomorrow. You c'n help me cut up my deer. Maybe I'll give *you* a haunch."

Roland shook his head dubiously.

Elvin had hunted out of season a couple of times over the past year. Somehow that little bit of illegal activity didn't seem all that terrible now he was on his own. Hell, a man had to have a little fun in his life, didn't he? And with this mysterious weight gain ("Must be my hypoid gland or something," he told himself), he knew his hunting days were numbered anyway. Another year and he'd have to get himself one of those crip carts, and wouldn't that be something? Meantime, he got around on his own feet but also kept a folding wheelchair in the back of the van for longer hauls.

Then, as he was on the verge of, well, he didn't know what he was on the verge of, but it wasn't good, that he found his salvation. It was at the gun show at the county fairgrounds, when he saw Her. The Swiss army knife of golf carts, her khaki and desert-sand paint gleaming dully, a whole load of gears and levers and fold-up-fold-down-hoist-up gadgets, all waiting to serve Elvin in his pursuit of licit and illicit game.

He had always been a frugal man, something Momma and Dot had praised him for. Despite his recent spate of caloric and alcoholic affairs, he still had a nest egg. He recognized that a big part of it had been the life insurance payout for Dot but reasoned that she'd want him to keep hunting as long as he could, to put that healthy meat in the freezer. Hell, it was an investment in the future. They'd be proud.

*

NORA SHIFTED HER WEIGHT ON her feet and peered hopefully up the drive to the Grace Woods Clubhouse. She'd worked a double shift; it was past her usual bedtime and her feet hurt. She stood in the shadow of a laurel grove that was tastefully planted beneath the live oaks surrounding the club. She wore the light green club shirt and dark trousers required for employees, and her coffee-with-a-hint-of-cream complexion softened contrasts, rendering her nearly invisible to the casual eye.

With a sigh she rocked back; the vehicle coming in wasn't Charlie's van either. Disappointed, she watched the dirty gray Ford van roll across the gravel drive and park halfway down the first row.

"Odd," she thought. At this late hour there were several empty parking spaces closer to the door of the clubhouse. Odder still, once the van was parked, gears ground noisily. The rear van door slid open and someone deep in the van's interior rolled a cart onto the heavy-duty wheelchair lift. More gears, and the lift sank to ground level. The hidden person apparently had moved to the front of the van and exited the normal way. Nora could see no other passenger. "If they need a scooter, why aren't they using the handicap spaces?" wondered Nora to herself.

Nora's eyes widened at the sight of the enormous man who came around the back of the van. He climbed onto the seat of the cart; it looked like a golf cart but there had been some sort of alterations to it, possibly to make it handicap adaptable? He steered it over to the far side of his van and clambered down. He not only left the cart resting there, but apparently, he intended to walk the entire stretch from his van to the clubhouse.

"What the hell?" she whispered to herself. She tried not to stare as the fellow labored his way to the entrance and went on in. She needn't have worried about his feelings; he was oblivious to her. Also, the elephantine man was already the worse for drink. Near as he was, she could smell it on him as he passed her.

Still no sign of Charlie. She shrugged and walked toward the van, curiosity piqued by the odd shape of the cart.

A closer look revealed that it definitely was a golf cart, but nothing like any she'd seen during her five years of pouring drinks at the Grace Woods Clubhouse. This thing had fat balloon tires, protruding machinery of a nondescript nature, and—

"Fucked up!" The thing was painted in camouflage! Even down here in lower Alabama, this was bizarre. She inched closer—a small key dangled from a twist tie around the gear lever. The guy had lowered this contraption to the ground, left its key, and gone on foot into the club with what was obviously great physical effort. "*Seriously* fucked up," she repeated to herself.

Another vehicle rolled up the drive. Nora looked up, waved happily. It was Charlie. Instead of walking over to where their family truck idled, she waved to Charlie to drive to where she stood. Charlie pulled over to her and rolled down the window. "Lazy," she scolded with her devil-may-care grin, "Couldn't walk the twenty feet to a parking space?"

"No, get out. You gotta see this!"

"Wow", whistled Charlie as she walked around it. "Camouflage golf cart. How screwed up is that? Was it here all evening?"

"Nuh-uh. This huge guy just pulled in a minute ago and lowered this to the ground. I thought he was going to use it like you know, a handicap scooter, but he left it, with the key right in it, and walked all the way over there to the door and went in. *Huge* guy. I think he was drunk. Smelled like a spilled six-pack."

"Think he uses it to play golf?"

"I can't see this guy doing any sport, except maybe watching a game on TV. I mean *huge*."

"Don't be sizeist. Maybe he can't help it."

"I'm not. Well, maybe I am. That stupid cart makes me despise anyone who would own it. It's like, the ultimate Bubba-mobile."

Charlie's eyes sparkled. "Let's take it for a spin!"

"What? No, you're crazy!"

"Let me park the car." Truck parked, Charlie hurried back. She hopped into the wide seat and grabbed up the tiny key left temptingly dangling. It slotted neatly into the ignition control.

"Charlie! Get out of there!" hissed Nora, looking nervously around the lot. All was quiet save for a small 'click' as Charlie found the gear to roll the cart forward. Tires crunched in the gravel.

"Don't just stand there, silly, get in!"

Nora, seeing a new pair of headlights coming in the driveway, shook her head despairingly and scrambled onto the seat beside her sweetie, who cackled maniacally as she drove the cart at a brisk clip past the side of the van and onto the dark links beyond.

"Don't roll this thing into any obstacles," muttered Nora, clutching the side rail with one hand and Charlie's arm with the other. "You're gonna get me fired, I just know it."

Charlie emitted a subdued whoop and turned the vehicle straight across the fairway, around a low clump of shrubbery. As her eyes began to adapt to the dark, she began to weave more confidently among the small traps and ponds that dotted the landscape.

"Damn," she muttered as they narrowly missed running into a pond. She stopped, reversed, and began to feel along the dash.

"What are you looking for?" hissed Nora.

"Lights."

"No! We'll be spotted!"

"I just need to switch them on every now and then. Aha!" She flicked a toggle. It appeared to Nora that the entire landscape was illuminated with a beacon that read, "Felons, right here!" The lights flicked off again. The landscape went black.

With a sharp turn, Charlie circumnavigated the pond, made another short dash, and drew up onto the soft grassy sward of hole #7.

"Wonder if there's a blanket back here?" muttered Charlie, twisting to reach behind her. Her elbow bumped a catch.

"Yow!" The women yelped in unison as the entire seat began to pivot on its base to face rear. They caught their balance. Nora giggled nervously and squeaked, "Surreal!"

Their feet now rested on what looked like an immense folded camera tripod. Charlie, feeling around in the dark, located a tarp. She hoped it was a tarp, anyway.

"C'mon," she said, scrambling out with her prize in her hands.

Nora stumbled after her and peered disbelievingly at her girlfriend in the dark.

"What, we're having a picnic on the golf course at 11:30 at night?"

"Yeah, babe," Nora could hear the leer on her sweetie's face, "And I'm the main course."

"Ah, sorry, I'm not really in the mood. Terror has that effect on me."

"Oh, come on, it'll be fun. You'll be glad tomorrow. You always are."

"Am not," Nora lied.

Too often, Charlie made her feel like the "straight man" in those madcap situation comedies, reluctantly but inexorably drawn along in the wake of the zany main character who drove the wrong way on freeways to jolly toe-tapping banjo music, egged on by a laugh track, emerging unscathed just in time for credits to roll.

Like that time. Hurricane Simone, roaring up the coast like a petulant child, kicking apart random beach houses as though they were yesterday's sandcastles, leaving others perfectly intact. The abandoned beach house, not yet bulldozed. Charlie, of course, had insisted on exploring. Across the slanted floor, shuffling through the indoor dunes, up a protesting staircase, Nora trailing behind also protesting.

The armchair set invitingly in the upstairs hallway. Charlie pushing Nora down into the chair, kneeling before her, opening Nora's shorts and peeling them down. Nora saying, "No, Charlie, how can I feel like it in a place like this? Someone could wander in any time."

Charlie looking up at her with laughing eyes. "Then we'd better hurry!" And wonder of wonders they had hurried, and it had been unbelievably intense and gripping. And satisfactory.

Remembering, Nora's lower belly contracted. Never mind that, indeed, shortly after Nora had rearranged her clothes and her tousled hair, a young man and his girlfriend had appeared at the top of the stairs and looked at them curiously.

"Place needs the wrecking ball,'" commented Charlie off-handedly to them as she preceded Nora down the stairs. Had they known? Nora thought so, but never mind. Yes, extremely satisfactory.

Charlie nudged her, probably remembering that time as well. "What's the worst that can happen?"

With an effort, Nora returned to the present. "What if the alligators are out roaming around?"

Charlie leaned in and rummaged the oddments in the back of the cart. "Gotta be a flashlight in here somewhere."

"How does that help with alligators? Make them stand up and dance in a chorus line?"

"Cute. No, you shine it along the ground all the way around you and if there are any in the area, their eyes glow—sort like a cat's. Red, I think. Or green."

"Oh." Nora edged closer to Charlie.

"Nope, no flashlight. Wait. I got an idea!" She pushed the seat face front and hopped back into the driver's side. She keyed the ignition. "Get in or get back, babe."

"Don't leave me!" Nora scrambled in.

"I'm not leaving." She flicked a switch and the lights glared out, laser-bright to their dark-attuned eyes. Nora winced and put a hand up. The rise of a hill, every blade of grass illuminated in sharp relief, filled the swath of light.

Charlie turned the wheel sharply and pressed the pedal. The cart swung in a tight circle, shining out in a 360-degree blinding arc like the grand opening of a cheap department-store.

"Wow!"

"See any gators?"

"Not for miles." Nora giggled. "Shut the lights off, silly, before someone from the club notices."

They climbed back out, retrieved the tarp which had been narrowly missed by Charlie's speedy rotation, spread it out and sat on its crackling surface. The turf, soft and smooth as a cushion-top mattress, gave slightly beneath them.

Still blinded from the cart's lights, they groped for each other.

"C'mere, you," muttered Nora, then "Ow!" as they bumped faces. She giggled again.

"I'm here." Arms enfolded bodies, lips met, and the tarp crackled obligingly as they reclined.

"Mmmm...." sighed Charlie. Engines rumbled in the distant parking lot.

"Wish we had some music," murmured Nora, who didn't like to be reminded of the proximity of strangers, even if those people were merely going home from an evening at the golf club, oblivious.

"I bet this magic machine has a radio—it has everything else." Charlie hopped up and hurried to the cart.

"Oh, come back. I didn't want you to get up, silly."

"Be just a second here. No, that's lights. Here, what's this one?"

A loud hum made them both jump. In the gloom, Nora could make out some sort of platform sliding smoothly out from under the rear bumper.

"Weird. It's got a shelf on the back. Maybe another tiny cart rides on *that*!"

Charlie chuckled. "And *that* cart has a little shelf, and a smaller cart rides on it...."

She found another control and pressed it. Out from the radio, loud enough to be heard by the inmates of the next housing project over from the links, boomed a cowboy with what sounded like severe sinus problems. He was explaining to them (and the nearby inmates) that Claire June had gone away and left him flat, with nothing but a six-pack and his hat.

"Jesus!" yelped Charlie and scrabbled under the dash to shut the thing off, choking the cowboy in the middle of a word that sounded like 'spoon' but might have been 'spitoon'. "Maybe I'll just sing to you instead."

"Come back over here, nut."

*

ELVIN PAID FOR HIS DRINKS and slid, with care, from his padded bar seat. Ankles, knees and hips felt the strain, but otherwise he still felt pretty fresh. This afternoon's siesta (and this evening's anesthetic; he'd lost count of the beers) had set him up pretty fine. He took a deep breath and turned to the door.

"Long walk to the van," he thought, but then: To the van, where the cart, *his* cart, his wonderful hunting chariot awaited him. He'd been tempted to park near the door, but he surely did not want anyone to notice his cart as he cruised into the tree line. He picked up his shuffling pace.

Get to the cart. Drive it off the lift. Wait, had he already done that part? Why would he have done that and left it unguarded? How many beers had he had before coming to the club? He couldn't remember.

Raise the lift, collect his rifle, and lock the van. Ride off the gravel edge of the parking lot, into the landscaped strip that delineated the lot from the woods around it. Ride grandly across the strip and into the woods, cruising silently on those big fat tires. Drop the camo-curtains and wait for Bambi.

Bag his deer, field-dress it, drop it onto the cart's shelf and glide triumphantly back to the van. Drive onto the lift, crank the lift up, pull the cart into the van, and home again, home again. Roland would have to eat his words.

Halfway across the gravel lot he stopped, confused. Must have left the cart inside the van? He shook his head, unsure, and resumed his breathless hike across the gravel lot.

Elvin stopped and squinched his bleary eyes at the empty lift and the van's open rear door.

"Shit," he breathed, and broke into what passed, for Elvin, as a run. Arms flailed, legs spraddled, breath rasped, and his pace picked up slightly. He leaned (well, fell) into the rear doorway of the van. No cart inside, no cart outside.

"God. Damn. It," he wheezed, proceeding to the driver's side. No cart in the lee of the van. Elvin stood, appalled. Call the cops? Explain why he'd been driving around with what was obviously a hunting vehicle, out of season? Have them smell his beery breath? No.

He staggered to the lift again and examined the gravel drive around it. The gravel revealed no tracks, of course. Could the thieves have loaded it onto their own truck and driven off with it? Or driven it away under its own power into the woods?

Despairingly he circled where he stood. No tracks. Nothing. He decided to drive up Grace Woods Road one way, then reverse course and drive the other way. Maybe he'd see something. He climbed into the cab of the truck, forgetting the lift that remained at ground level on the rear.

Key in ignition, he paused. There, way off across the golf course, a light flickered sideways like a beacon. Two lights, in fact. Golf cart lights? Why the hell would someone be driving a golf cart in a circle, on the golf course at night? The lights disappeared abruptly. He leaned out his window and squinted into the distance where the lights had been. Darkness enfolded the landscape again, the links appearing as gray velvet.

He sat, considering, hand on ignition key. Then, through his open window floated a few bars of a country song that was popular at the moment.

"Shit," he rumbled, "I hate that stupid song." The song choked off mid-word. Elvin blinked. The music had come across the golf course, not from any nearby vehicle. He was sure of it.

"Why in the *hail*...."

Elvin breathed deeply, two bull-like snorts through a nose long reddened by years of overindulgence.

"Those punks," he growled, and started his truck.

*

CHARLIE PAUSED AND LIFTED HER head.

"Mmmm, don't stop now, you were doing so well," purred Nora. Then she, too, froze.

The vehicular sounds came closer. The lovers stared across the links; where the engine's roar originated, a shape eclipsed the lights of the clubhouse. The shape veered left, swerved the other way, and bounced high. No lights on the vehicle; it was just a noise and a big ungainly form roaming the landscape like a mastodon.

A mighty splash informed them that the primeval beast had found a pond and, apparently, found it less than good. A string of curses floated richly to their ears. Gears ground. Tires howled as they spun for purchase in mud. More gears, more tire sounds and then apparently the tires gripped drier ground. More gears; the mastodon now loomed closer.

Nora grabbed her shirt and groped for her pants. "Oh god, Charlie, I'm gonna lose my job," she gabbled, hopping on one leg as she tried to dress.

Charlie had pulled on her socks but the shoes still eluded her. "Where'd they go? Dammit, where—oh, here's one...." Scrabbling sounds. "Hey, it's okay, babe. You dressed? Let's go."

Charlie got to her feet, one shoe on her foot, one shoe in her hand. She grabbed Nora by the other hand. "It's every man for herself!" she yelled exuberantly, and then in direct contradiction to her words she hauled Nora behind her and set off toward the nearest shrubbery.

"That doesn't even make sense!" panted Nora. She put on a burst of speed and was now dragging Charlie. They dove into the clump of bushes and squeezed through to the other side.

"I know, I've just always wanted to say that. Oooch!" said Charlie as a branch snapped back into her face. They sprinted to another rough patch closer to the woods.

"You punks! Kill you!" The mastodon seemed to have found its target and also its voice. It wheeled over a rise and, horn blaring, bore down on the luckless golf cart.

The lovers turned and gaped through their new shelter. "Better not be snakes in here," whispered Nora. Charlie knew that there probably were but kept quiet on the subject. They peered back at the scene of their "picnic" in time to witness a gray Ford van looming out of the dark, wheelchair lift dragging off the back gouging up green velvet furrows as it came, plowing broadside into Elvin's magical hunting cart. The women winced.

"Shit," rumbled the mastodon. The horn ceased. The driver's side door opened, and a huge figure slowly slid down. It reached back into the van and toggled a switch. Headlights came on, illuminating the ruins. Elvin stood, baffled, blinking drunkenly at the carnage.

The two women edged carefully from their covert, keeping it between them and the man. Floodlights switched on at the rear of the clubhouse. Shouts floated across the links from that general direction. The hubbub moved out onto the course and eventually made its way to Elvin, his van, and the wonderful hunting cart, now folded nearly in two by the impact.

Nobody noticed Nora and Charlie as they sauntered with extreme casualness to their family truck. They waved cheerily to the incoming sheriff's car and sedately departed down the driveway for home.

*

ELVIN HAD HELD UP PRETTY well during the initial period of sitting handcuffed among the ruins of his hunting cart. The local law enforcement debated whether he could be charged with DUI for driving on a golf course (while it was not a public roadway, it *was* public property) or merely with public intoxication and vandalism. He'd maintained an outward appearance of calm during the standard "vandalism and mischief" lecture from the security guard of Grace Woods Golf Club. Thoughts of Roland's ridicule made him hyperventilate only slightly.

What broke his heart, though, was the moment (coincidentally, at the same moment that Charlie and Nora fell happily naked into bed, still exhilarated by the evening's adventures) a Grace Woods employee brought around a Grace Woods golf cart to carry Elvin back to the Grace Woods parking lot. Mortified, he climbed into the gaily colored seat of the cart, which sagged under his weight; no reinforced suspension here! Its gaily colored awning flapped merrily in the breeze as the cart labored back to where the sheriff's car awaited him. Elvin was a broken man. He wondered if Dot and Momma would talk to him ever again.

*

THE CLUB HAD CLOSED, EXCITEMENT over for the evening. The last tow truck had departed, the Swiss Army Knife of golf carts dangling like a gutted deer carcass from a hook in back. A lone doe stepped daintily to the edge of the woods and watched as the final employee's taillights winked out at the end of the driveway. Possibly, the doe winked back.

As we were driving south on I-65 in Alabama we passed a truck pulling a trailer with a golf cart on it. This golf cart, however, was painted and bedecked in camouflage, as though this particular golfer didn't want anyone to notice his (of course we assumed the shy owner would be male, right?) presence on the course. "Going to play a few stealthy rounds this evening?" we chortled. Which of course led us to the title, which of course led me to Elvin.

THAT WOMEN'S
MUSICAL FESTIVAL

FRIDAY

HAROLD'S MAD AT ME BECAUSE I have to work overtime again this weekend. It's only another conference. He knew I'd have to work this one because Janelle filled in for me last week cause of Harold having another one of his attacks. He just never remembers, I don't know how come.

Don't tell Harold, but I mostly like working the desk for these littler conferences. Not so much those big business ones, where all those loud-talking men with their cell phones and laptop computers and those Raspberry and I-Pod things come and boss us around and need special fussing-over, but the little ones where just families come. Or I like these even better, when just ladies come to enjoy themselves doing something they like to do.

Like, take that one last month when the Longaberger Basket ladies came for a weekend. They were all just the nicest gals you'd ever want to meet, and they had the best time.

There was this one little lady, she must of been about sixty, I think she was Eye-talian or one of those other ethnic things, but so what if she was? She was just as nice, and she showed me this darling basket she had for her little baby granddaughter, I forget her name, the granddaughter that is, but it had the cutest little angel doll wired to the handle, it looked like one of those fancy artistic Precious Moments figurines. I always wanted to collect those, but Harold says they give him the fidgets.

So anyways, this weekend there's this bunch of ladies coming here for a festival, something with music. I never heard of it before but it's a pretty big deal, a national festival. I hope they'll have some really famous musicians like Dolly Parton, but I just don't know yet. We've already registered about fifty of the ladies, and they're just so friendly, it seems like they all know each other already. They all went to chatting together right there in the lobby and making plans for dinner before they even went up to see their rooms!

And here's a funny thing, I think a lot of them must be sisters because they didn't even care that there's only one bed in their room. I know lots of the really big acts are related, like the Judds and them, so maybe it's not so funny after all.

At first, I didn't care for one or two of these ladies, they seemed kind of, you know, *mannish* to me. I even thought that some of those mannish ladies were boys, at first, but Heddy (her real name's Hedda but all her friends call her Heddy), who works the front desk with me a lot, laughed and said I was just so 'out of it' and that I should get with the times. She teases me but I don't mind, I know she's just in fun. She's nearly young enough to be my daughter but we're good friends anyways.

Oh, I know that lots of women wear pantsuits and blue jeans these days, but these women musicians wear outfits and cut their hair and walk in that straddle-legged way just like boys. For a few minutes I wondered if some of them might be those awful Gays you hear about, but I've seen the parades on the news, and none of these gals walked around with no shirts or carried signs with dirty words on them or stuck their tongues in each other's mouths. I don't believe any of them came here on a motorcycle either.

In fact, once you got past how they looked they were about the nicest, friendliest group of gals you'd ever want to meet. Some of 'em would look right pretty if they'd fix themselves up a little, but instead they stride around all bold and mannish like their mothers hadn't ever taught them a thing about how ladies should act. Maybe it's because they're all musical performers and it's part of that artistic temperament you hear about. I'm not sure. But I sure hope that Dolly Parton gets here pretty soon. When I tell Harold about that maybe he won't be such an old poop about me working this weekend.

SUNDAY

WELL! HERE'S ONE FOR THE books and no mistake. Heddy got two tickets for the big Saturday evening show. They call it "The Main Stage" which is silly to me, that makes it sound all flat and boring. Anyways, Heddy wanted me to go with her. Heddy's been divorced for a couple of years now and I know she must be really lonely.

Harold kicked up a fuss about me going, even though I offered to buy him a ticket so's he could come too, and he said he'd rather stay home alone than watch a bunch of women caterwauling up on a stage. But I said, "Harold, don't be an old poop. You know that poor Heddy's all alone in the world and we're blessed to have each other and our health and we should be happy to help out the less fortunate."

I didn't even remind him that he never pays any attention to me when he's watching those police shows on TV anyway. Then I made him the tuna casserole with crushed potato chips baked on top and Velveeta cheese just how he likes it, so he stopped his grumbling. He's really an old softie.

Then, he's such a peach, (our anniversary is coming up, and I found a coupon for Applebee's in his trouser pocket when I was getting them ready for the cleaners, so I know he plans on taking us somewhere really nice), he says, "Now honey, don't stay out too late or I'll have to find me a new girlfriend," in that twinkly way of his.

So anyways, Heddy and me went to the Main Stage show. The most surprising thing was almost the whole audience was ladies! Seems that not all of the ladies staying at the hotel are performers after all, they're friends and maybe sisters of the performers. And lots of other gals from around the area and even two states away came to watch the show too.

When those Sweet Adelines were here last September, the audience was full of all kinds of folks, husbands and kids and all, but these performers didn't have any of their families there to hear them, just an auditorium full of women. I felt so sorry for them, poor things, but they all seemed really happy, so I guess they didn't expect any better from their families. I'm such a lucky girl, I just know that if I was to ever get up on a stage to perform, my Harold would be right down there in the front row and both our grown kids and their families too. Well, maybe not my daughter-in-law Susie, but I won't say another word on *that* subject.

The first act was a bunch of foreign girls, all banging away on drums and a xylophone-looking thing and some big rattles with beads all over them, and pretty soon most of the audience got to singing along with them and waving their arms in the air and such. The sound was all echo-y and they sang all over the top of one another so I couldn't really understand what they were singing, although most of the audience seemed to know or maybe they were making up their own words.

"This is almost like a tent revival," I whispered to Heddy, who was clapping along with the music. She just laughed and went right on clapping.

The next act was a lady called Chris Williams, she had real short hair and funny clothes but of course nobody seemed to mind and by now I was getting used to it myself. She played a guitar, and sure enough, the gals around me started singing along.

Then I realized what a silly I'd been! Because what they were singing was a hymn. It wasn't one I knew, but it was one about how we'll walk on the water and be cradled in the deep while angels sang us to sleep, a really pretty song, and everyone swayed back and forth as they sang and smiled at one another.

Then Mrs. Williams sang about an endless waterfall filling up and spilling over, which of course was a parable, and all the gals were holding hands and swaying and just filled with the spirit. Naturally it was a little unusual to me, us Methodists are a little quieter in our worship, but our church was invited once to the colored Baptist church downtown and this Main Stage service was a lot like that one, with everyone clapping and dancing around.

So of course, that's why all the husbands and boyfriends and all stayed home, this was a women's retreat. I didn't understand a lot of the songs and the speeches (the amplifiers were awful loud and blurry sounding), but everyone around us laughed a lot and called out things.

At the intermission, Heddy met one of those boy-looking gals in the ladies' room and struck up a conversation with her. Jody, the gal's name was, lives right here in town. Heddy introduced us and I asked her what church she belonged to. She said Episcopal. You know, before now I thought Episcopalian folks were more sedate in their services, like the Methodists, but everyone has to move with the times, I guess.

We didn't stay for the whole Main Stage service, it just went on too late for us working girls, but we both had a real good time and I had lots to tell Harold when I got home. He was disappointed about me not seeing Dolly Parton or the Judds, but it tickled him when I sang him a little bit of that waterfall song.

TUESDAY

HEDDY SAYS THAT HER AND Jody met for a coffee after she got off work yesterday, and they're getting to be real good friends already. I think that's real sweet, her and Jody can keep each other company and not be so lonely since neither of them has a husband yet. That festival retreat was just the ticket for poor Heddy!

Whenever we're attending National Women's Music Festival and register at the hotel, I wonder what the hotel employees really think of the gay, mad clientele that descends on them. I know, our narrator is exaggeratedly sheltered and insular, but who among us hasn't met someone pretty close to this lady?

LAST TENDER TO BLUE-MOON BAY

Sunday, at the airport:

I almost gave this blank book back to Nadine after she crapped out on the trip and got nasty about it, but I've decided to show her that I'm bigger than that. I can't believe it, her getting all "poor me" just because her hours got cut back and she's making less and leaving me stranded on the cruise except for Thea and Eleanora.

Of course, I had to confront her about it directly, I just hate it when people get all passive-aggressive and then sulk about stuff because the other person is clueless. So, I told Nadine how inconsiderate it was for her to change her mind about going along. I mean, you only go around once, and money's just a scorekeeper when you look at it, right? So, she says sarcastically, "Sure, I can still go—you going to loan me the ticket money?" What a bitch.

But I'll be fine. I'll mostly hang out with Thea and Eleanora. And I'll journal the cruise just like we were planning to do together and read Nadine the good parts when I get back, to show no hard feelings.

We heard that some people cancelled the trip because they're worried about that fever outbreak thing, and one of the women in the airport said she was afraid they'd cancel the whole cruise because of that. But nobody we know has any of the symptoms so it's probably just one of those news stories that's way overblown. CNN says it's like that ebolo thing you read about in horror stories except this thing gets spread by casual contact. I think they're just trying to blow the thing up, to sell newspapers.

So here goes, getting on the plane just in time. We already saw several lesbians taking this same flight, how cool is that!

SUNDAY, ON THE SHIP:

WE GOT BOARDED OKAY. TURNS out some of the passengers did cancel at the last minute so Len and Thea got the balcony they wanted. I'm in a BIG solo room! Score! It is so fun to be on this giant ship with all the lovely lesbians, not to mention the entertainers that we usually only get to see if we go to a big festival. Gotta get to the pool and order myself a couple of margaritas!

MONDAY:

GETTING THIS SHIP FIGURED OUT. I had to explain about Port and Starboard to several women, but then I got lost myself a couple of times so it all evens out. Man, it's true what people say about cruises, you could eat yourself to death on these things. Drinks are extra and I'm going to have a HUGE tab at the end, but you can have pizza six times a day for free if you want, and don't even ask about the ice cream machine. The crew folks keep making us use that hand-sanitizer, seems kind of rude but oh well, don't want to get that stomach bug people talk about.

I was watching TV this morning, they have a ship channel with one of the comedians saying what's going on each day and some interviews and stuff, it's kind of cute. There's also CNN so you can see what's going on back home, but that's sure not much fun when you're on a cruise. The CDC issued a bulletin about that epidemic, they want people to not travel unless they have to, and avoid crowds, yadda yadda, like every flu season. Glad we're out here on the ocean away from that!

Tonight, we're having a mixture of comedy and music. That concert last night was *crazy*. Nobody was supposed to save seats, I tried to keep a couple for T & E but you know they're always late, so I just met them afterward for drinks. They said tonight they're not staying up as late, party poopers. I'll go to the after party by the pool—maybe I'll meet some cool gal-pal, LOL.

TUESDAY:

OMG, I THOUGHT THE SHOW was <u>so</u> great. Never laughed so much in my life, nearly peed myself, but Eleanora said it wasn't as good as what she expected. She's not usually so negative!

Thea says Len's worried about her sister. Carolyn lives in Miami, and I guess the outbreak started there—probably came in on some freighter through the airport there or maybe that cruise port. Anyway, Len's been up at the internet cafe a couple of times a day (costs extra, what a rip-off!), making sure Carolyn's okay, but she's not. I think she just has a flu or something, but Len says she has a fever and some aches and pains, which is how this ~~hemhorragic hemorrhagic~~ this plague thing starts.

I've been trying to tell her to be more positive. Of course, if she's going to think the worst it will make it happen, but she got really bitchy when I said that. Oh well if she wants to be that way. The steward was late yesterday doing my room and I had to complain.

I sat in the dining room at one of the Solos tables and met some cool women. One, Val, is a retired teacher but lots younger than you'd expect—she said she saves her pennies so she can do one of these women's cruises a year, a different destination each time. If you go on enough of them, you get some super-star status and get primo seating in the theater and other stuff. I tried to "invite myself along" with her, ha ha, but she didn't get the hint. Oh well, who said all teachers are smart? She was kind of cool anyway. I'll try to sit at her table tomorrow night; she's easy to spot, tall and has bright red hair.

Tomorrow, we go to Blue-Moon Bay, we don't dock there but ride in on ferries. Tenders, they call them. You have to get in line early so you'll have enough time on the island. It's all private beaches and you can sign up for private cabanas (expensive!) or shade things. Thea and Eleanor and I were going to share a shade thing but Len's not sure she should come ashore. It's not going to make Carolyn any better for her to sit around and worry, I said, and she said (in a *so* really bitchy way!) "What the hell do you know about it?" so I don't think I want to share the shitty canopy thing with them anyway. Thea already paid for the whole thing, and she can just eat the whole cost if they're going to be that way. I thought they'd be a lot more fun to travel with than this.

I thought the service on this cruise would be better, too. As much as we paid for it, the food should be a lot better, and the help isn't as friendly as they were the first day. On Sunday we had two stewards for each section of rooms, but I've only seen the one the whole entire time since then. He comes in wearing a face mask, looking like a Martian and sprays this stinky chemical stuff around. I asked for fresh fruit in my cabin and it took him a whole day to bring it. Service was really slow in the dining room, too, and I never did get the second drink I ordered.

I went down to the main desk to complain, but there was a HUGE line there. Some of the women were there about Blue-Moon Bay activities, but mostly it was people asking for service of one kind or another. There was only one person at the desk, and he looked really cranky and obviously wasn't much help. I gave up after about half an hour waiting. When I went by later, there wasn't anybody there, in line or behind the counter.

WEDNESDAY:

BLUE-MOON BAY WAS OKAY, BUT it took forever to get one of the tenders. Never did see Len and Thea but I spent the day there with this really fun couple, Jan and Dee. They were on the bench opposite me on the tender, and when we got there, they were fooling around at the entrance where the photographer takes pictures. There's a hot pirate babe who'll pose with you, and Jan and Dee had everyone in stitches, pretending to be in love with the pirate babe and fainting in each other's arms and stuff.

A couple of other singles and I joined them and did some group shots. We bought a couple of bottles of rum at the shop and kept ordering fruit juices and mixing our own recipes. Wow!

Jan said someone told her that there's a bug going around some of the crew and that's why the service is so bad all of a sudden. It's not that plague thing of course, which CNN says is spreading around the coastal areas and a mess of people have died (mostly really old folks and little kids). But we have the flu or something going on and it's making for some lousy service. Just our luck!

We were one of the last groups to go back to the ship—everyone was sort of in the bag by then, but we ate some dinner anyway. It wasn't all that great; either half the stuff on the menu had already run out or something, and the waiters acted like they didn't even give a shit. Hardly anyone was at the show tonight and half the performers were ROTTEN. Some didn't even show up. We ought to get a discount for this whole cruise, it's really starting to suck.

Still nobody at the main desk, I don't know what the deal is there. Supposed to be 24-hour service.

Anyway, the rumor is that the crew is really nervous about the flu thing and we're still sitting outside Blue-Moon Bay and it's nearly midnight. Don't know what the holdup is but if we're going to get to Barbados on schedule, we're really going to have to book it!

THURSDAY:

STILL SITTING OUT HERE IN the Bay. I'm really getting pissed about this. Eleanora and Thea aren't answering their phone, either. I knocked on their door, but nobody answered. It sounded like someone was in there, but kind of muffled, like they were seasick or in the bathroom or something. I've decided I'm not going to waste my time on them, let them come to me when they're good and ready.

Jan's one of those people who is really good at finding stuff out (she used to be in the Army, in security). She says that flu thing has spread around really fast and they're afraid we won't be able to dock at any of the foreign ports. That or the plague thing has hit the ports and they're afraid we'll catch it. But since the Blue-Moon Bay is a private place for the cruise company they can come and go to it. We tried to get on one of the tenders going back in there but those stupid guys in uniforms made us get away from the gangway. Can't tell who's going on the tenders from here, but it's not anybody I recognize—maybe just crew people.

It's getting hot in the cabins too! They keep turning the A/C back for longer and longer times. God-damn patriarchy—I bet if all the passengers weren't lesbians, they'd treat us better. If it's going to be hot like this we should at least be able to go to the beach.

THURSDAY LATER:

WE WENT UP TO THE Lido Deck and watched, and some passengers definitely DO get to go into the island. It might have been the special needs women (I guess it's okay if they do that just for them), they all looked like they needed to be helped. One of the comedians was down there, that tall Latina one with the spiky hairdo. I should be better with the names but was kind of shitfaced Monday night when she was on. I didn't know she had accessibility issues. Jan and I yelled down, but she didn't hear us. I think she was really drunk, she stumbled getting on the tender and puked over the side. It looked red, like she had too many Bloody Marys. Gross.

Jan and I ordered a bottle of tequila, and it took *four hours* for it to come, and we had to go upstairs for ice. There was hardly any ice left, I had to really dig around to get any from that little bin. It looked a little nasty but the alcohol will kill the bugs! LOL!

Jan said Dee was feeling kind of crummy, Jan thinks she's just really hung over, says she feels kind of pukey and her eyes are all bloodshot. Too much fun in the sun!

They closed the dining room, and everyone has to eat at the buffet on the Lido Deck. Food's really looking stale and picked over. We better get a HUGE refund when this is over. If I get sick from the bad food or water, I'm going to really be pissed off.

FRIDAY:

MAN, THIS IS REALLY STARTING to creep me out. Jan went back to their room and Dee was just gone. No note. I helped her look everywhere, and we haven't found her yet. We stuck a note on the door for when she comes back, but no luck so far. I thought maybe they'd had a fight and Jan was just being clueless (we've been pretty wrecked part of the time) but she says no, Dee wouldn't just disappear like that. Dee's more the yelling type she says.

We've been asking every uniform guy we see (they're all wearing those face masks now), practically, but they just shake their heads like they don't understand. Doesn't anyone on this boat speak English? Man, I'm SO ready to go home, this just sucks.

More tenders go to the island, and it looks like they're taking lots of laundry there in those big canvas cart bags on rollers. There's no food or anything on the island except what comes in the ships, so I don't know why we don't just turn around and go back to Jacksonville. Or "back to the world" as Jan says, from her Army days!

SATURDAY:

STILL NO DEE. JAN JUST sits and cries. She thinks Dee fell overboard and nobody cares.

No more A/C on the whole ship, and not many lights. Hardly any meal service, and most people are staying in their rooms. Only time I see rooms open is when the crew guys are cleaning in there, and they give you a dirty look if they catch you trying to look in to see if anyone's home. Getting to be like a ghost ship!

Plus, I've knocked on Thea and Len's door several times and nobody answers, no sounds in there. The crew guys just shrug and look dumb when I try to get them to open that room.

SATURDAY AFTERNOON:

MY ROOM STINKS. WHEN I flushed the toilet, some crud came up in the bathtub. Red like blood, but it smelled like shit. Can't find any of the crew guys to report it. It's like zombies or something, there's hardly anybody around. I brought this journal and came up to the pool in the back and a couple of women were lying in the deck chairs, asleep. I said kind of loud, "Hey, anybody know if there's a show tonight?" and one woke up a little bit and sort of mumbled at me and then went back to sleep. A military-looking helicopter went over, don't know where it came from, but it just kept on going.

SATURDAY NIGHT:

NO LIGHTS IN MY ROOM, which smells worse than ever. The whole ship stinks. There are a couple of lights on, here in this lounge. I think I'll sleep here. Jan didn't answer her door. I saw Val, that hot redhead, in the stairway (elevators are dead). She had one of those stupid masks on but she was still pretty easy to recognize. "Val! Are you okay?" I said, and she turned around and RAN, I swear to god. Like I was a vampire or something. I tried to run after her, but she was faster.

I went back up to the pool and the same women were sleeping in the deck chairs. I think they might be really sick. I almost went over and tried to wake them up but I was afraid to, I don't know why. It even stinks up there on the open decks. My head hurts. Can't find Jan. Guess Nadine was right to stay home.

SUNDAY:

IT'S NOT LAUNDRY. GOD, IT'S not laundry in those carts. I saw Len, down on the tender. She was screaming, just screaming. Two uniform guys were running the tender and two others wheeling the carts around. They tried to make her let go of the laundry cart but she wouldn't. She climbed in it and grabbed a bundle and just screamed. They left her in there. They let go the ropes and the tender just went off toward the island with Len and the carts and it never came back.

SUNDAY NIGHT:

MY GUT HURTS. MY EYEBALLS ACHE and we're just sitting here. I wish I could go to Blue-Moon Bay.

We, along with several of our friends, had saved our pennies for a once-in-a-lifetime Olivia cruise and of course we had a magical time. One of the shore excursions was for a day of fun in the sun at the cruise line's private island. As we lined up for the tender ride back to our cruise ship, someone mentioned that it was the penultimate shuttle, and that the last tender from

Half-Moon Cay was usually filled with younger, inebriated partiers. One of our friends said, "'Last Tender from Half-Moon Cay'; that sounds like the end of the world. It would make a great story, wouldn't it?" So of course, I had to write it. A few days after we'd all arrived safely home, we began to hear the news reports of a Carnival ship stranded at sea and the miserable time the passengers and crew were having. I wrote this story well before COVID struck, but I'd like to think that a ship full of lesbians would be able to pull together and cope with such a circumstance, but one never knows....

FAIR EXCHANGE

ANDREÉ STARED INTO THE MIRROR, frozen with shock. It certainly wasn't what she was used to seeing when she looked into mirrors. If she thought about it, (which she certainly didn't now, she was too stunned) the first time she'd been this fascinated with her reflection she'd probably been about six years old. Six, yes, and mesmerized by the sudden vacancy next to her upper front tooth.

Not long after that, she'd lost interest in her image. It was always the same, a skinny little girl with long hair, braided or pulled into pigtails tied with ribbons of various colors. A girl in ruffly new Easter dress of tender pastel color, prim in patent leather shoes and white gloves (with a dime for the collection plate, pushed down into a glove finger as far as it would go, so she wouldn't lose it). A girl in a sophisticated black velvet jumper with embroidered white blouse at Christmas.

She must have been a cute little girl. Andreé remembered times when, overcome by childhood grief or outrage, she'd begun to cry and her mother telling her, "Oh, don't cry and spoil your pretty face!"

And of course, Andreé had cared not a whit for her pretty face. She had pleaded as she grew older, for her mother to cut off the hated pigtails. She had only ever seen one girl with short hair (it was called a "pixie cut", as she recalled) but she knew immediately that this, if she couldn't get a buzz cut like the boys, was the haircut for her.

"What was it with moms and their daughters' hair?" she'd mused to Carolyn, "Every butch I know seems to've had a mom who gave her Toni permanents or fancy little updos when she was little."

"They all do it," her wife had told her, "Primate bonding or something."

"Huh. Maybe so. I think my mom stopped liking me when I finally started cutting my own hair."

"Oh, stop. Your mom likes you. In her fashion."

"Yeah, but not like when I was frilly."

The adult Andreé, finally secure in her own butch identity, adopted the hair and clothing she'd only dreamed of in her middle-class girlhood, and she no longer felt the desire to avert her eyes from the mirror.

She felt she'd come to terms with the mirror. She and it didn't fuck around. She could walk right up to it and check out the state of her teeth (trapped granola bits?), her face (sunburn peeling yet?), her clothing (did that coffee spill wash out or not?) In fact, Andreé and her mirror had been perfectly content for the past 35 years, until this morning.

She stared. Raised her right hand. The bimbo with the streaky blonde do and the pouty pink mouth raised a matching hand. She touched her face, thinking vaguely of Harpo Marx as she did so. The bimbo did likewise. Well, maybe not a bimbo as such. The apparition was probably an ordinary heterosexual teenage girl, looking about sixteen to seventeen years of age if Andreé was any judge of such things, which of course she wasn't. All teenage girls looked like hookers these days. All the magazine covers attested to that.

"Brit? Hey! The second bell's about to ...."

A bell exploded into sound outside the door. Andreé jumped. She looked around vaguely at the girl in the doorway, who gestured impatiently.

"You talking to me?"

"Who else? Brit? What's wrong?"

"Brit? Who's Brit?"

The girl, nonplussed, gave a sigh, and shifted her weight to her other hip. "You can dick around in here if you want; I'm going to class." She turned and sashayed out the door.

Andreé looked around, noticing from the corner of her eye that the horrid doppelganger did so as well. She was in what looked (and smelled—this brought back decidedly non-nostalgic memories of her own high school days) like a high school restroom. Lipstick prints on the walls. This had always perplexed her; who would want to kiss a wall in a public restroom? Disinfectant smell slightly masked the "toilet overflowed, and we didn't clean it up very well" odor. Scabrous mirrors from which the silver backing had flaked away for too many years to consider. Stall doors with graffiti.

She looked and wondered. She hadn't wakened in her own bed this morning; at least she didn't remember having done so. Of course! A dream, but one more vivid than usual.

"You always have such interesting dreams," Carolyn often said, with a hint of wistfulness. Carolyn never remembered her own dreams.

Andreé stood, patiently, staring at the bimbo, who stared back. She sighed. The bimbo sighed. Could you get bored in a bad dream? She'd better wake up before she found herself in a car, speeding up the cables of a suspension bridge and preparing to plunge her 300 feet straight down into Lake Michigan or something.

Unaware of how much she sounded like the woman in *Rosemary's Baby* (*pixie cut*, she mused with one part of her brain), she said aloud, "This is no dream. This is really happening!" The bimbo mouthed this along with Andreé.

"What the hell is happening here?" She felt for the cell phone in her pocket. No cell phone. No pocket, for that matter. A purse bulging, she saw, with various items of makeup and a hairbrush clotted with long hairs (the bimbo sneered in disgust at this), stood on the edge of the stained and pitted sink. To hell with it. Andreé poked gingerly through the purse. No cell phone.

"Gotta call Caro—see if I'm there."

She left the purse on the sink and turned, nearly tripping. She looked down and saw herself. Young and (she looked back up, horrified anew), young and stacked, that was the word. Ash blonde. Dressed in the most skimpy and impractical garments she could imagine and teetering on flimsy little plastic shoes with little plastic heels.

"There'll be an office. They'll have a phone."

Wobbling on the plastic shoe-ettes, Andreé left the restroom.

*

"Eeeeeeeeeeeee!" The throat-ripping train-whistle shriek blew Carolyn (Caro to her friends and her wife) from a fitful "time for the alarm to go off" sleep. It was a sound she would never forget, and it was coming from the throat of her nearest and dearest.

"Andreé? What—?"

"Ohmigod! Who are you? Where is this?" gabbled Caro's partner of 20 years. Caro shook her head, still nearly paralyzed with sleep and adrenaline overload.

"Sweetie?" She looked around the room for what could have so horrified her level-headed wife. Nobody and nothing there, and only now did she realize that Andreé was staring, mouth and eyes wide, at her. Carolyn ran a hand down her face. No gushing blood, aliens, dangling snakes or spiders seemed to dribble from her ordinary morning face.

She reached a hand toward Andreé. "Dearest? Andreé?"

The woman in her bed jerked away from the hand as though it was poison. "Stop calling me that! Don't you come near me! Are you a terrorist? Am I a hostage?"

"Sweetie, stop this! You're scaring me!" Carolyn reached again toward Andreé; dammit, she didn't want to cry, but....

Andreé shrank back again. "What are you? A lesbo?"

Caro tried for another explanation. Andreé had been known to indulge her wry humor in some fairly over-the-top flights of fantasy; this was extreme, but who knew?

"Dearest, if this is a joke, I'm not following and, I'm sorry, it's just not funny. Maybe it has something to do with being scared shitless by thinking something's hap—"

The face on the woman in Caro's bed changed and now Carolyn felt like screaming. She'd never seen a look of such vapid craftiness on her partner before. The face, a stranger's face, looked around.

"A joke? Is that what this is? Tiff? Cassie?"

Carolyn, at a loss, reached one more time toward Andreé's shoulder.

"Don't touch me!" spat Andreé, backing away convulsively. She then fell spectacularly off the bed, hitting the floor hard. Air whooshed from her lungs.

Caro got out and ran around the bed. "Your back!" Then she groaned inwardly as she heard herself utter the cliché, "Are you okay?"

"When this is over," she thought, "We'll have a good laugh about this."

Five years before, they'd both hit a patch of ice on a sidewalk (warm spring rain, still-frozen ground), Caro landing like a runner sliding into home plate, Andreé flailing wildly and falling half-on, half-off the concrete. Caro had staggered to her feet and asked, "Are you okay?" whereupon Andreé, despite her pain, had breathed out a laugh, "No! How could anybody be okay, after that?"

They'd sworn, for future accidents, to ask something more sensible.

"Do you need me to help you?" she asked now, reaching a hand out, even as she knew what this would do to the hysterical female who was and wasn't her partner.

Andreé scrambled clumsily up and backed away. She bumped against the open closet door and shrieked again, a shrill, drilling sound that hurt Carolyn's ears, and then spun around.

When she saw her own image in the full-length closet mirror, she screamed a third time. "What have you done to me?" she howled. Her hands flew up to her face and pulled down. The red insides of Andreé's eyes glared back at herself in the mirror.

"Am I in a nightmare?" she whimpered, "I want to wake up. Please let me wake up!" She sank to the floor and wailed, rocking back and forth.

Carolyn sagged back onto the bed and sat still, staring at the crumpled figure. Possible explanations wandered through her mind. Instant onset dementia? Stroke? Demonic possession?

"Know what happens if you don't pay your exorcist?" Andreé had asked her not long ago.

"No, dearest," Caro had patiently responded, "What happens if you don't…."

"You get repossessed!"

Carolyn had obediently groaned.

Now her lower lip trembled, and she wiped a tear away. Barring death, she'd never been able to imagine anything happening to the two of them that they couldn't handle with grace and humor.

The figure on the floor had quieted somewhat.

"Andreé? Can you try to tell me what's going on?"

"I don't know! I'm not Andreé. I don't know any Andreé! I'm Brittany!"

"Brittany?" In Carolyn's childhood, Brittany was a type of spaniel. Had Andreé been saddled with a name like Brittany, she'd have hied herself off to the local county clerk's office and changed it as soon as she'd come of age. You could make Andreé from a girly name like Andrea, but what could you do with a spaniel name?

"Yes! Brittany Keisler! And I don't look like this! That's not me! That's old, and it looks like a lesbo!" Andreé-Brittany jabbed an accusatory fingernail at the mirror, and for a horrible moment Carolyn could see the virtual press-on nail that a Brittany would be wearing.

"Am I a hostage? Have I been drugged?" After a silence while she drew a shaky breath, Brittany-Andreé demanded, "Is this identity theft?"

Carolyn nearly laughed but didn't. Then she took a deep breath and reminded herself, "I've been teaching fourth graders for the past two decades. I can handle this."

She squared her shoulders and spoke firmly to the moaning figure.

"I want you to calm down. Get up off the floor and sit down over there."

The figure obeyed her.

"Now then, 'Brittany', I want you to tell me whatever you can about yourself. Tell me your birth date, where you live, names and ages of your family members, whatever you can think of to describe who you really are."

If Carolyn expected the delusion to break down at this point, she was disappointed. Dumbfounded, she sat and listened to her partner, in the ungrammatical but rollicking jargon of the modern adolescent, recite an encyclopedia of detail about one Brittany Keisler, born October 12, 2007, in a suburb of Pittsburg, PA, to parents Janet and Scott Keisler, now divorced. She listed friends, boyfriends, enemies, favorite television shows and least favorite teachers at West Union High. She was willing to share her cell phone number, her login ID and her locker combination, but not her social security number because, "I, like, have a right to privacy, don't I?"

*

THE TELEPHONE RANG EVEN BEFORE Carolyn had marshaled her thoughts as to what she'd say when she called Janet Keisler's phone number. She answered it cautiously.

"Caro? Dearest?"

Through the receiver Andreé's voice sounded higher, strained, but it was definitely the voice and inflection of Caro's one true love. Carolyn began to sob.

"Where are you?" she managed and was not terribly surprised to learn that Andreé was calling from inside the body of a teenage girl in a high school in a Pittsburgh, PA, suburb.

*

"BRITTANY" DISSOLVED INTO TEARS WHEN she heard her mother's voice on the telephone. "Mom? Mommy? I'm in Chicago, and I'm old and ugly!"

Carolyn itched to slap the girl, but instead she returned to her room and got dressed. She went to the kitchen, made herself a bowl of cereal and sat down at her computer, spooning raisin bran into her untasting mouth as she looked up airline flights to Pittsburgh.

She packed a bag for herself and one for Andreé-Brittany, allowing Brittany to select what she deemed the least reprehensible clothing items. Caro drove them both to the airport, parked the car in long-term, and submitted herself and her companion, now in shock or permanently immersed in Teenage Sullen mode, to the prove-yourself-innocent humiliations of airport security.

"When I was your age," she told her uncaring companion, "They used to warn us in civics class about how repressive things were in the USSR. They told us that citizens there were treated like, well, pretty much the way we just were, and that's why we had to fight like hell against Communism." Brittany rolled her eyes.

Caro's jaws ached from clenching them by the time the plane arrived at Pittsburgh. Not that, at the best of times, she'd have enjoyed sitting cheek-by-jowl with strangers, barreling through the air in a pressurized aluminum tube. Somehow, though, it was so much worse to be accompanied by Andreé's body encasing this kvetching little airhead.

What happened between elementary school and high school? she wondered. The fourth graders had their issues, certainly, but she loved them for their bright alertness, their curiosity and ingenuous, if sometimes silly, conversations. Alas that this, this *person* (her mind shied away from thinking of Brittany as a young woman, though sadly, that was what she was, gray hairs and love-handles notwithstanding) had lost the best part of her youth in such a short time.

As directed, they proceeded to the baggage claim area for the next phase of this surreal day. Brittany squealed and launched herself at an unknown woman nearly twenty years Caro's junior. The woman, already not at her best, stiffened with shock as the body of a fifty-five-year-old butch lesbian hung around her neck, sobbing and wailing. To her credit, after the initial recoil, she relented and awkwardly put her arms around the foreign body from whom her daughter's words and sobs tumbled.

Caro felt eyes on her and wrenched her gaze from the painful sight before her. A teenage girl near Janet Keisler stood, in Andreé's posture. Andreé, when caught doing something foolish or embarrassing. Andreé, head down, looking up from beneath pale eyebrows and a tumbled mass of ash-blonde curls. She was remembering...

College: Andreé's editorial about the need for a stoplight at a dangerous pedestrian intersection on campus had just won second place in the state-wide journalism competition. The awards banquet was that night, and Andreé's roommate, in full Pygmalion mode, was helping her prepare.

"Just let me," she said firmly, pushing aside Andreé's warding-off hands, "just a little touch of blusher. Oh, you look great! You should do this more often! Stand up, see how great you look!"

Andreé, with an internal shudder, beheld herself. Indeed, she did look fine, for a girl, that is. She was slender, elegantly attired in white "shell" top and black straight skirt that showed her legs to fine advantage. She wore low-heeled spectator pumps (she'd drawn the line at the higher ones), her short glossy dark hair swept up behind and glued into place with hidden hairpins and a lot of spray.

"I should be in a drag show," she thought to herself. "Just walk down the hall and back," urged the roommate, "get used to the shoes."

Obediently, Andreé clomped down the hall and back. She hated how she felt, how she looked, and it showed in her walk, her posture and even, she felt, in her skin.

"Andreé?"

"It's me. Up to a point. Caro...."

The voice Caro heard was higher than Andreé's; it was the one she'd heard on the phone. No matter. If she closed her eyes, Caro could hear her beloved, or someone doing a very good imitation of her. She took three steps toward the child before her, closed her eyes again, and held the apparition, rocking as they crooned their private endearments.

When she opened her eyes, she beheld Janet Keisler's glare and could read the thought, "Take your filthy hands off my daughter, you pervert!"

Janet Keisler averted her eyes from the distasteful scene. She too felt the need to close her eyes. Her daughter's voice was hoarse, but through the hoarseness she recognized her own.

"Brit? How did this happen?"

"I don't knooow.... How can I go to school looking like this? Oh, mommy, I just want to *die*!"

Caro looked away from the shell-shocked mother. Closer to her ear, however, Andreé whispered, "Dearest...." Caro closed her eyes again and rocked the girl in her arms as the Andreé-girl murmured, "We'll get through this. I'll cut off this stupid hair and start working out. Why is it that my whole life I keep having to cut off a mess of hair?"

"I woke up to this, this *siren* in my ear, and there you were, next to me, or so I thought...."

"Horrible! Just horrible! You can't imagine. I opened my eyes and there was this—

bimbo in cheap ill-fitting clothes, looking at me from a mirror. I was back in *high school*!"

"... and that woman over there kept thinking *I* was her girlfriend!" babbled Brittany to her mother.

Airport passers-by ignored them, busily jockeying for position around the revolving luggage-o-matic.

*

ANDREÉ, STILL MORTIFIED IN HER new body, snuggled against Caro. The last three months had been a blur of lawyers and bureaucracies, and the red tape nightmare wouldn't really be over until "Brittany" turned 18 and the Social Security Administration could be brought to heel. Maybe never, come to think of it.

They'd managed to get through the days after "swap day". There were outbursts of hysterics and angry accusations, mostly from the Keisler family; lawyers were brought in and countersuits threatened.

Eventually, Andreé returned home, the fingernails clipped off, the hair shorn, the miniskirt and heels traded in for a pair of jeans and sneakers. She was gradually coming to terms with her new body, that of a young, handsome butch jock, leggy and now developing muscle mass.

Brittany, however, was Brittany. Caro shook her head ruefully. Apparently all the poor child had enjoyed in her life was being blonde and thin. Returning to high school in a fifty-five-year-old dyke's body was not to be thought of. Under cover of the tale of a critical but non-fatal illness, she was being homeschooled until her hair grew out and the braces began to move Andreé's appealing crooked grin into something more conventionally 'pretty'.

*

"MY POOR OLD BODY, I feel such pity for it," confided Andreé. "Imagine its being face-lifted, liposuctioned, starved, and made to walk around in high heels for the rest of its unnatural life. Like driving an elderly horse beyond its endurance until it collapses."

"Don't worry, it will rebel. You know it will. Foot cramps, lumbar spasms, bruxism…. How long do you think she'll tough it out before she buys a pair of sensible shoes?"

"I give her about a month."

Andreé smiled wryly and continued, "I can see that I got the best of the deal as far as longevity, assuming that body age goes with the body. But what happens when Brittany dies? Will she shoot back into this body? If I died, would I return to my own body?"

Andreé chattered on, free-associating ideas as though the whole thing was an interesting sci-fi story. Caro froze; what, indeed, *would* happen? She shook her head to clear the image and held her dearest tightly. Nothing, she reminded herself, could happen that the two of them couldn't handle. At least, she fervently hoped so.

I had this dream. I have no idea how it would work out in real life, but insanity is likely to be part of it. What is it in our world that makes such a ruin of teenage girls' self-images?

ALAN THOMS

LAINIE GLANCED TOWARD THE COFFEE shop window again, and then looked away again. The boy was still out there, just as he had been since she'd noticed him ten minutes ago. A pink band-aid stood out sharply against his dark cheekbone, belying Johnson & Johnson's claim of their product being "flesh-colored."

He was small and slim, and the solemn look on the narrow mahogany face reminded her of herself at that age. There the resemblance ended. She sat in the coffee shop, sipping her latte and eating her croissant. The little boy's earnest gaze made her feel unaccountably white, stout, and wealthy.

She wasn't, of course. Not by today's standards, anyway. Her weekly coffee date with Brenda was something of an extravagance, fiscally and calorically. The little boy at the window had no way of knowing that. She stole a look and found him still watching. He tapped rhythmically on the glass, then on the pavement, with a furled light blue umbrella. The bus stop shelter beside him was empty save for the glittering foil of an empty gum wrapper. The child, in fashionably faded jeans and a Marvin the Martian t-shirt, seemed clean and neat and lacked the bold, crafty look that Lainie had learned to expect of streetwise kids.

"He has a musical sense, anyway," remarked Brenda, "I find myself tapping my foot along with him." She smiled and waved to the child, who simply continued to stare.

"He's gotta live around here, doesn't he? But it does seem early for a child that age to be out and about. Where are his friends?"

"And does his mom know he's out there, staring into the windows of shops? My mom would've clobbered me for doing that."

"Maybe he's autistic or something. Well, I can't say this particular coffee date has been all that fun compared to most of 'em." She smiled at Brenda. "That kid's sort of creeping me out."

"Don't give me that. What he's doing is worrying you."

"He just doesn't seem to have a grownup anywhere around him. Doesn't he seem too young to be out alone, early in the morning?"

"He does." Brenda, even as she agreed, was gathering up her purse, "Work calls, sweetie. I'll see you tonight." They walked outside, kissed, and separated, Brenda walking to her car and Lainie toward the sidewalk around the corner in front of the shop.

"Where are you going? Oh, Lainie, no, leave the kid alone. Lainie?"

She scurried after, grumbling and shaking her head. By the time she got there, Lainie stood over the child, looking down. He stood, sturdily holding the umbrella before him, one hand at either end of it as though creating a barricade between himself and the hefty white woman standing over him.

"What's your name, son?"

"Alan."

"Alan what?"

"Huh?"

"I mean, what's your whole name?"

"Alan Thoms."

"You mean Thomas? Or Thompson?"

"I 'on't know."

Lainie tried to remember whether she'd known her own last name at that age. She thought she had, but then she hadn't been allowed to hang around bus stops alone, either.

"Do you live near here?"

"I 'on't know."

"Well, where *do* you live?"

"With Mama."

"Can you take me to your house?"

"Uh-uh."

Brenda thought for a moment. "Where did you sleep last night?"

"Here."

Nonplussed, they stared at the child. Here? In the Something's Brewing Coffee Shop? In the bus stop? In one of the low brick apartment buildings across the street?

Brenda got another idea. "Can you point to where you slept last night?"

Wordlessly, Alan pointed to the bus shelter.

"You slept in there? Alone?"

"Mama and me. We got a ride with a man. She gave me her 'breller to take care of, and we went to sleep. She gone when I woke up." His lower lip trembled; manfully, he controlled it. "She coming back soon."

"Alan, what did you have to eat today?"

"Nothin'." The lip quivered again, ever so slightly. Again he controlled it.

"Come on—let's get you some breakfast." Seeing him hang back, she reassured him, "Just inside there. So we can watch for your mama through the window."

"Are you crazy?" hissed Brenda, "Picking up a strange kid and offering him food? You know what people will say, about a couple of white lesbians picking up a little kid, no matter what color."

"No, what will they say? That we eat other people's children?" Lainie stared defiantly back at Brenda, who flushed, but held the look steadily.

"Well anyway, you don't even like kids," Brenda muttered to her, under the hum of the early-morning commuters.

It was true. Lainie avoided children, not liking their noise, their rude shovings and grabbings, and the unconcerned way they had of putting their fingers in disgusting places and then into their mouths or onto something she was about to pick up.

She herself had grown up on a farm. Life was serious. She'd gone to school with children and, presumably, played with them, but most of her memories were of chores, worries about the weather, and how the bills would be paid. She'd thought of herself, when she had at all, as part of a team, or a small corporation. Modern children seemed so frivolous, as though their only job was to be children. The young Lainie would have scorned a job like that.

This youngster, though. He didn't seem like a child so much as a small trapped feral animal, with a wild animal's dignity and resignation masking the desperation apparent in his eyes.

"Well, I don't especially, but we can't just go off and leave him here like this. Things happen to kids."

"Well okay, let's get him something to eat and ask the clerks if they know him."

Alan followed them through the door, holding his umbrella. Lainie stepped up to the counter and surveyed the menu. "I'd like one of your breakfast croissants, with bacon and cheese. Oh, thanks, sweetie," she added to Brenda, who plunked a small container of milk onto the counter beside her.

"Is he yours?" The clerk, who'd seen them nearly every week for the last couple of years, looked slightly surprised and, Lainie thought, disgusted. Why? Because he was black, and they were white? Because they were obviously gay, and this wasn't their own child?

"Well, no. He seems to have gotten," she realized that Alan was easily within hearing range, "Uh, separated from his mom. She'll probably be back any minute," she added hastily, fearing tears.

"She'd better hurry up, then. That kid's been looking in our window since I opened at 6:30. At first, I thought he'd just missed his bus. Kind of young, though, to be riding the bus alone. So, he's not yours, hey, that's a relief. I hated to think you're the kind of folks who'd leave a kid standing around all that time, unsupervised."

"Alan? How old are you?"

"Five. Goin' on six."

"Practically grown up," agreed the clerk, and seeing where Alan's eyes had been fixed as he spoke, reached into the glass case and brought out a chocolate-chip cookie. "On the house," she added in response to Lainie's doubtful look.

"It wasn't the cost. Just, won't it spoil his breakfast?" She looked at the boy and shrugged. "Guess not."

She paid for the food, and indicated with her chin the table where, ten minutes ago, she and Brenda had sat in uncomplicated comfort. "Let's sit there, Alan, so you can watch for your mom."

Unselfconsciously and systematically, Alan put away the food. A bite of the cookie, a drink of the milk, a bite of the croissant, then back to the cookie. He was surprisingly deft in his habits, stopping mid-bite to pick up a dropped chunk of cheese egg that had fallen to the tabletop. He popped it into his mouth, mutely accepted the offer of a paper napkin and wiped first his hand and then the table with it.

When he finished eating, Lainie concluded that some of the boy's fastidiousness had, mostly, to do with hunger. Not a crumb remained in front of the boy. He sighed, and then returned his eyes to the bus stop outside the window.

Brenda looked at her watch, shook her head, stood up.

"Yeah, you'd better get to work, babe. I'm sorry I made you late."

"Don't be silly. I'm going to call my boss and tell him I'll be an hour or two late." She ignored Lainie's blatant look of gratitude and pulled her cell phone out of her purse.

Lainie excused herself to Alan, who acknowledged the courtesy with a quick glance before returning his gaze to the window. She waited until the coffee shop clerk finished ringing up a scrawny student in a t-shirt bedecked with airborne lobsters. The caption read, "Lobsters in flight—only at the Good Table Restaurant."

The t-shirt steadied her. "I'm not the only one who's crazy," she thought.

"Have you ever seen this little guy before? Around in the neighborhood?"

"Nope, he's a new one. Listen, hadn't you better call someone? The police or something?"

"I suppose so. I hate to do that, you know? You see stuff in the papers, little kids left behind in Laundromats and at the sitters, and you think 'They ought to take that kid away forever'. But then, take the kid away to what? Brenda's sister works at a shelter and has nothing good to say about Children's Services. Understaffed and overregulated, and the kids lose no matter what."

"Well, you can't just leave him here. That sounded nasty, didn't it? I didn't mean it that way, but wow, you know?"

"Yeah, I know. Sweetie?" She reached for Brenda's cell phone. "I need to call in too. Be right back.

Brenda returned to Alan's table and took a deep breath. "Alan? I think your mom's going to be, ah, delayed for a while."

"Huh? You know where my mama is?"

"No, I mean that it might be a little while before she can come back."

Where was the blasted woman? Dead in a ditch somewhere? Shacked up, a smoldering crack pipe on the dirty floor next to the mattress? Eaten by a shark? In the emergency room, frantically trying to describe to an attendant where she left her little boy while getting change for the bus and having a heart attack?

"She be here."

"Well, but it might take a while. She might have gotten…."

The Band-Aid on his right cheekbone bunched up as his little face stiffened.

"… busy," Brenda amended hastily, "She might be really busy with something. She won't want you just hanging around the bus stop until she gets back."

Alan looked interested. "Where we go?"

Lainie rejoined them. "What? We're going somewhere? Do you think that's such a good idea?"

"No, you came in on the tail of the conversation. Nobody's going anywhere."

"Well, we can't just leave him here. Alan? Do you have any relatives around here? Your grandma? Auntie? Daddy?"

Mutely, he shook his head. Then apparently realizing something more was required, he elaborated, "Grandma, she dead. JoJo, he went away. Long time ago. Then we come here in that car, and that man left us here."

"Honey, we're going to have to call someone to help you find your mama. We don't know exactly where she is, but the police...."

"No!"

"Alan...."

"Don't call no police! Mama din't do nothin', I din't do nothin', don't call 'em...."

His low-level terror now rose and washed over him. He put his hands, hampered by the umbrella, over his face and wailed. The clerk stared, shifted uneasily, and then looked away.

When Lainie was 10 years old or thereabouts, her father had given her responsibility for a calf that had been born blind. As the animal was weaned and the mother began to drive it away, the calf had more and more difficulty with finding good grazing.

"Might as well hand-raise her for a while, fatten her up and we'll put her in the freezer next year," said her father.

Lainie knew better than to grow attached to an animal destined for slaughter, but the heifer imprinted on the girl's smell and voice and began to follow her around the barnyard. Against her better judgment, Lainie named it Helen Keller, first as a joke and then because she admired the handy way both Helens navigated through their dark world.

A year later the stock truck pulled into the yard. Lainie, nearly blind herself with hot tears, led the trusting beast up the ramp and into the smelly interior. When Helen tried to follow her back down the ramp, Lainie slammed the tailgate, nearly on the startled animal's nose, then turned and ran behind the barn. She'd sworn to herself that she'd never eat any of the meat from the neat white paper-wrapped bundles in the freezer. Now, nearly three decades later, she wondered if she'd stuck to her vow. She simply couldn't remember.

She looked at Alan who'd trustingly followed them indoors and laid his fate into their hands. Not the same thing as Helen, not at all. But of course, that's how it felt.

He rocked and sniffled quietly. Lainie handed him a paper napkin. He scrubbed his nose without comment. Lainie took another napkin and wiped a stray tear (she hoped it was a tear) from his cheek.

"What can we do?"

"I can't help thinking of the scene in *David Copperfield*, when he shows up in his Aunt Betsy's dooryard."

"Oh yeah. She said, 'No boys here!'" Her voice rose in a cackling imitation of the elderly Dickens spinster, startling a chuckle from the boy.

"Well, but she has that demented boarder, remember?"

"How did that go?" Brenda shared Lainie's fondness for classic literature, especially the schmaltzy stories, "'Mr. Dick. Here's this boy who's run away. What shall we do with him?' And Mr. Dick says, 'Why, I should wash him!' But Lainie, we can't just take him home like a stray pup. This isn't Victorian England anymore."

"I know."

An hour later, Alan sat in front of the television watching a video of How to Train Your Dragon, a bowl of popcorn in his lap, content in the knowledge that a note had been left at the coffee shop. His mama, when she came back, would know exactly where to find him. Half an hour later he slept, and he stayed asleep as Brenda's sister stormed in.

"Are you nuts? Do you know what they'd do to you if he falls out of a tree and breaks a leg or something? What's going to happen when his mom does come back and yells bloody murder about the white busybody lesbians who kidnapped her child? Or worse, if she doesn't come back at all? You planning on raising him in the attic or something?"

"What could we do? Leave him there?"

"You have until this evening to call Children's Services, Sis, or I'll do it.

"Okay, okay! Do me a favor, first..."

"No!"

"C'mon Trace. I'm just asking you to talk to the kid when he wakes up."

"Damn it."

That evening, Alan, minuscule in the queen-sized guest bed in his brand-new dinosaur pajamas, clung to Lainie, tears on his cheeks. The tears had come more frequently as day walked into blue twilight. Lainie assumed that was to be expected. The umbrella poked her ribs. She didn't notice it.

'Cn' I stay here until Mama comes?"

"Alan, we're going to try very hard to make that happen."

"No! You say!"

"Alan, we'll try. We can't just do whatever we want to."

"Yeah, you can. You white. And you rich." Lainie sighed. "I wish we could do just what we want. We'll do our very best to help you find your mama, and we'll try to keep you safe here with us until we do."

It was enough. As though Lainie'd flipped a switch, Alan slumped in her arms. His eyes closed. She quietly laid him down. The umbrella slid from his hands and lay beside him in the bed, as Allen Thoms slept.

One sunny Friday morning we'd made our weekly coffee stop on the way to work. We noticed a little boy standing alone outside, looking aimlessly in the coffee house window. Despite the clement weather, he held an umbrella. No adults appeared nearby, and we began to wonder if he were perhaps lost or abandoned, and what we would do about that. At that point a bus rolled up and a woman stepped out from behind the adjacent bus shelter, took the boy's hand and boarded the bus.

TRASH TRAILERS

ALICE HUNG UP THE PHONE and sighed. She did love her mom, of course she did. But, she reflected, Mom didn't always make that easy.

"I had a thought," she'd said with hope in her heart, "you have everything you need at the St. Pete condo now, so we don't really need to drive all that way this fall. I can just make two plane reservations and we'll fly down in style, how'd that be?"

"Couldn't possibly," snapped Mom, "You know how awful it is to deal with these airlines nowadays. In style?" She punctuated this with a hyena-like sound.

"Oh, it's not that bad," Alice tried feebly, "We won't go during a busy time. Maybe I can find a direct flight; wouldn't that be better than two days in a car?"

"Now, if the trains still ran," ruminated Alice's mom, "We used to take the Zephyr Express to the capital every spring. The Pullman cars were very well-appointed." She sighed heavily. "Of course, nothing is as it was."

"No," her mom concluded firmly, "It's best we drive. We can stay at that nice hotel outside of Knoxville, the one with that sweet little colored girl who makes the omelets at their Sunday buffet."

African American woman, corrected Alice, but only mentally. "Mom, I have to go feed Elmo. I'll check back when I know what days I can get off work for the trip."

"Now, don't forget to have the car overhauled."

Tuned up, corrected Alice mentally. "I won't, Mom. Talk to you soon. Bye now."

It wasn't that Alice's mom was a bad travel companion. She knew how to read a map and give plenty of warning when a tricky interchange was coming up. She knew when to hold her peace when Alice made wrong turns or missed exits. She knew how to peel a banana and hand it correctly to the driver.

"The trick," explained Mom, "is to look at the driver's hand and not at the road." She chuckled. "My, the time it took for me to learn this. Your father used to get so *mad* when I poked him in the face with one. 'I'll watch the road, that's *my* job', he'd sputter."

The very basic issue was that Alice didn't like to travel at all. She loved the idea of travel, and in fact subscribed to magazines that showed laughing tourists toasting one another in exotic settings, elegant hotel rooms on platforms above crystal-blue lagoons, beaming uniformed servitors holding trays of colorful foodstuffs on the sidelines. At home in the evenings she'd stroke a purring Elmo and flip through the pages of these magazines, secure in the knowledge that she wouldn't have to actually take herself to Iceland, Costa Rica, Bora Bora or Moscow.

Delivering and fetching her snowbird mother to and from St. Petersburg, Florida, was the extent of her peregrinations, and she then returned home like a homing pigeon, gratefully landing on her assigned perch and settling back in.

Resignedly, she requested a week off from work and had her car serviced.

"Elmo? C'mon, Elmo. It's not so bad. They give you treats, remember?"

"Owowowowoww," yodeled Elmo as he took his short ride to Dr. Robertson's Pet Hospital to be boarded.

*

"ALICE! WHAT ARE YOU DOING?" Her mother, Alice thought, had been dozing, but now she was espresso-awake, reaching for the dash with her patented "Mom in a panic" clutch. Alice didn't let up on the gas pedal.

"There's a giant SUV that's halfway up our as… up our tailpipe. I need to get past this truck before it runs us over."

Mom hadn't slept well the night before. She never did, in motels, she claimed. (But she ripped off some pretty good buzz-saw rasps and snorts most of the time Alice lay awake, Alice noted but did not mention.) Mom was cranky.

"You should allow plenty of time for passing, Alice."

Alice gritted her teeth as she pulled back into the right lane sooner than she preferred. The SUV driver, face obscured by the bill of his baseball cap, blared his horn and added a one-finger salute as he blew by. The cap's bill appeared to stare at her face. Odd.

"How rude!" commented Alice's mom.

*

"ALICE, LOOK! IT'S THAT RUDE man again!"

Alice followed her mother's pointed finger across the rest area parking lot to the same silver SUV that had so aggressively passed them earlier. The driver was nowhere in sight, but the bumper stickers proclaimed his temperament clearly enough. "God hates fags" was the mildest of the lot, followed closely by one that described the former U.S. president's wife as being slightly below humans on the evolutionary scale. (Although, as another bumper sticker pointed out, evolution was a liberal fantasy.)

What Alice had earlier mistaken for dice or some religious icon (her attention drawn, as it was supposed to be, to the rude gesture), was actually some sort of unclothed doll dangling from the rearview mirror, a noose around its neck. Alice shivered.

"Mom, don't point," Alice murmured, looking around for the driver.

"Of course not," huffed Mom, "*Some* of us have manners."

*

"Mom? Mom, wake up. We're nearly at the exit."

Alice's mom blinked and sat upright. "Oh, good. I'm just ravenous for some of those homemade dumplings and chicken."

Alice stifled her opinion of the particular chain restaurant in question, whose politics mirrored those of the van driver and whose menu favored "homemade" this and that although none of the ingredients had ventured near anybody's house except in take-home clamshells. The folksy atmosphere was enhanced by a row of rocking chairs on the back-home-style front porch, and the entrance to the dining area led through a dizzying array of kitsch, tchotchkes and brick-a-brack for sale.

"... and I just love those little Hummel figures, they have on display, well, they're not really that brand, but there's one that reminds me of you when you were five...."

So of course, they ate there.

As Alice and her mom departed and prepared to drive the short distance to their mid-range motel, Alice noticed a silver-gray SUV tucked away at the end of the row they had parked in. From this angle she was unable to discern what bumper stickers it carried. Likely it wasn't the same vehicle at all.

"Mom? Isn't that...."

"Alice! I wasn't finished talking! What is it?"

"Sorry to interrupt, Mom. I just thought...." She shook her head. When you travelled you sometimes repeatedly saw the same vehicles or other travelers on the same route. She assumed it had been this way, back to times when caravans of camels wound through wayside oases to and from the Far East with spices and silks. "...I saw a flock of redstarts," she finished lamely.

*

"NO, REALLY, THIS IS GETTING ridiculous," thought Alice. A whole day later, taking the exit to Pass-a-Grill Beach, and there was that silver SUV *again*. Or was it? Two cars behind them, and didn't all those petroleum-sucking behemoths look pretty much the same except for their color? Something dangled from its mirror. Maybe. Maybe not.

"Alice! This isn't our turn!"

"Oh Mom, you're right. I just thought this might be quicker," ad-libbed Alice. Now they sat at a dead end, facing the beach. A green and yellow bird darted across the low dunes between clumps of sea oats. In the rear-view mirror, Alice watched the silver vehicle roll by the intersection. Definitely a doll-like figure hanging from the mirror. "Gotcha!" she thought. After a moment, she backed out of the cul-de-sac, and they proceeded to her mother's winter apartment building.

"Mercy!" said Mom as they climbed out of the car, "I thought we'd *never* get here!"

*

ALICE STAYED AT HER MOTHER'S condo as planned. Longer than she'd planned, as was typical. She tried again.

"I'd better leave now if I want to beat the rush-hour traffic."

"So *soon*?"

"Mom, you know I always like to make an early start."

"Well, dear." And she sighed, quietly and patiently, "I'd hoped you'd help me with these trellises this morning, before you left."

Alice bit back her exasperated reply. She should have expected this delaying tactic. She should be touched that her mother was so reluctant to part with her for these few winter months. So many of her friends at work told stories of parents who never seemed to even want their grown children around. She was lucky.

But Alice did want to leave. And she didn't want to drive after dark to make up the lost hours. It always gave her the willies, to be on the road alone as the sun set, not knowing where she'd be staying that night. She had one of those little purse-sized pepper spray things, somewhere in the bottom of her purse, but somehow that never made her feel any more secure.

"Okay," she said as chirpily as she could manage, "Let's get those trellises installed."

"It won't take any time at all," said Mom happily.

Alice tapped stakes into the dirt and tightened screws, while her mother kept her company.

"Alice?"

"Yeah, Mom?"

"Don't say 'Yeah', dear. It's so common. I was wondering whatever happened to that nice Elaine? Do you still hear from her?"

"Oh yes," answered Alice vaguely, "We exchange cards at the holidays."

"She's married now, isn't she?"

"No, don't you remember? She found herself another— roommate," said Alice, whacking a stake with more force than was necessary.

"Mercy on us! Be careful! You didn't hurt your hand, did you?"

"It's fine," lied Alice.

"I always liked that Elaine," said Alice's mom.

*

ALICE ALWAYS ENLIVENED THE RETURN trip with audio books. She had once tried to interest her mother in listening to them together on these trips. Mom had been genuinely offended.

"What? My company isn't good enough for you?"

"Mom, it's not a personal attack. I just thought you'd enjoy a good novel while we rode along."

"If I wanted to read, I would do so."

"You get car sick."

"Nevertheless."

They'd ridden along in silence for a while after that and so now Alice saved the audio books for her solitary trips home. She immersed herself happily in the latest one.

"Ruth stops smiling and her face turns earnest. She pulls her leg away, sits up...."

The creepy guy in the creepy SUV hadn't been in evidence during the last three days at Alice's mother's apartment. Obviously, Alice decided, some of the sightings along the highway had been coincidence and the others might not have even been the same person. Anyone could have been driving those SUVs; there were thousands like that all over the country.

Imagination, of course. That was always her problem. Alice's tastes in reading did include the occasional stroll down the dark side, with Koonz and King to remind her that things could Always Be Worse. She always wolfed their novels down avidly once she got started, though afterwards, as the sun bent toward the westward horizon, she wished she had left well enough alone.

Salem's Lot. Now, that one was certainly an issue of misplaced timing. She knew she shouldn't have read that during that time after Elaine had moved out. For weeks after the final line ("Fire is purifying"? Was that how it went?), she'd gone with reluctance to her perfectly clean and well-appointed basement, strictly during the daytime, to do the laundry.

Worse, she'd dreaded sundown and the night to follow. Getting to sleep, an ordeal even before reading that terrible, wonderful story, took an eon every night. If you lay awake in the dark, she knew, and stared at an open bedroom door, sooner or later it moved. You could tell yourself it was an illusion, that the night before it had also appeared to move in that same way and when blessed daylight had finally arrived the door had been in exactly the same position it had been when you retired, but dammit, this time the door *had* moved. And so on, night after night.

Of course, it never actually had and eventually other, more uplifting books had managed to banish the terrors of Straker and Barlow, and sunset.

But of course, Alice's lively imagination could always give her a fright when she allowed it off its leash. It was clear that the baseball cap guy with his dangling doll had almost succeeded in untying that tether. She took a deep breath and muttered, "Get hold of yourself."

Then, since her wandering mind had missed the last minute or two of "Talk Before Sleep" (beautiful writing! She wished she had such loving and attentive friends as that), she tapped the Back button and replayed the last minute.

*

TIME HAD CERTAINLY GOTTEN AWAY from her. She'd hoped to get as far as Knoxville, where a very nice Hilton beckoned. One of these years, she mused, she should book a night at the Peabody in Memphis and take her mother there. It would be worth the detour to see the ducks, silly as the idea was.

Instead, here she was not even to Atlanta, among the lesser motel chains and fast-food signs, and the sun was just past that maddening spot where it blazed into her left eye and no hat brim or sun visor would help. Alice sighed and began to study the green "lodging" signs at each exit.

When she found an exit with four motels, she checked her rear-view mirror (strictly for safety's sake, of course. Not looking for any silver SUVs, oh no, because of course there were lots of those on the road, she had noticed scads of them this very day) and switched to the right lane.

She saw one motel on the left, looking a little shabbier than she liked. The other three lined up in a row on the right, backed up against a hill. She chose the farthest in the row just because it looked freshly painted, and checked in.

Alice hoisted her suitcase to the folding rack, washed her hands, and inspected the view from her window. The hill rose steeply behind all three motels. Her room, quietly situated as per request, well away from ice machine, staircase, swimming pool and busy roadway, faced this hill. In a row along the hill were three establishments marching off to the right: medical building, now empty and locked up; Golden Steakhouse restaurant, jumpin'; and behind her own motel, a graveyard of abandoned trailers. Or maybe a staging area for new trailers, ready for delivery?

Alice wasn't sure, but they were identical metal-sided boxes like she'd seen on construction sites. Block blue letters read "Metro Trailer" and a phone number. Empty windows like blank moony eyes stared back at her in the dusk. She could see the undercarriages of the nearer row of trailers—some had tufts of pink insulation poking through the sheet-metal underbellies. okay, so *not* new trailers.

The field was huge, unfenced, and appeared deserted. Alice counted; fifteen of the small ends of the rectangles faced the sliding window in the back of her room. Alice pondered. Hard to tell from this angle. Five rows? Ten? It didn't really matter. One deserted trailer was discouraging enough. Hangout for wayward teenagers. Hiding place for shopping mall zombies. Ditto for vampires. Alice cursed her overactive imagination.

Ah well, she was checked in. Her stomach rumbled. She closed the curtains, screening out the dismal landscape, grabbed her purse, and strode briskly to the reception desk where a young man was poking at his smart phone with a stubby finger. "Hi, I'm Brandon!" his name badge informed her.

"Where's the nearest restaurant that's clean and serves healthy choices?" she inquired.

"Oh, that'd be the Golden Steakhouse, just up the hill," said Brandon, "You can walk there in five minutes if you want to. Just turn left out the front door, cross the parking lot and go along that side road there."

Alice complied cheerfully, but then she realized that the side road bordered the field of those blank-windowed Metro trailers. She stopped at the edge of the parking lot and stared doubtfully at them.

They sat like a Shirley Jackson house, silently looking back at her (... *and whatever walked there, walked alone*, her mind commented helpfully). Traffic on the main road a block over honked and bustled. Alice considered getting into her car and driving out to the main road, navigating a left turn in the traffic, and driving two blocks to park in another lot.

"Don't be ridiculous," she scolded herself, "It's still broad daylight." It wasn't really, but the crepuscular air was mild and surprisingly fragrant. Also, she needed the walk. She set off on this short stroll. No sidewalk, but then few cars travelled this back road.

"Perfectly safe," she told herself. Nonetheless, she stopped and opened her purse. Wallet. Hairbrush. Pocket-sized pepper spray bottle? No, that was the hand sanitizer. Ah! She fished out the pepper spray and tucked it into the side pocket of her fleece jacket.

The Golden Steakhouse, it turned out, was a buffet of the kind where you pay a set charge, grab a plate and let your appetite and your obese children run loose. There had been a similar one in the small town her family had moved to when she was younger; after one visit her father had dubbed it "the Hog Trough" and they almost never went there. ("You're such a classist," Alice had playfully scolded him, and he had looked pleased.)

*

"Rats," she muttered as she left the Golden Steakhouse. The 'broad daylight' of before was now full dark. Still, shafts of light leaked from the rear of each motel and ground lighting illuminated the tall boxy yews clustered thickly around the deserted medical building up ahead. The quarter-mile walk back to her motel should be safe enough.

A light wind kept any mosquitoes at bay. Alice felt brave and adventurous as she swung out of the restaurant parking lot onto the road.

Nonetheless, Alice glanced nervously around as she walked. Traffic noise filled the air from the fronts of the motels, but back here all was quiet. Nobody seemed to use this road, at least not after business hours.

Peaceful, she told herself. Not spooky. It felt good to be out of the car and using her own body to transport herself. She resolved to be more active when she was at home. Silly, really, to hop into the car and drive the few blocks from house to store. She could carry a few groceries in a backpack; after all, didn't small children walk to school wearing packs half their own size, and those packs stuffed full of heavy textbooks hanging off their little shoulders? She had certainly been turning into a lazy slug lately. Well, no more! In fact, maybe tomorrow morning she would take another walk along this road before setting out for home...

Her wandering gaze stopped; likewise her feet. "Huugggh!" Alice thought she knew what it was to be afraid. When her bedroom door seemed to move on its own in the night, she'd feel her heart speed up, breath become short and shallow, sometimes a dizzy feeling even though she was lying down in bed. Now, though, she nearly choked on terror, intake gasp of air fighting with exhaled "Oh!", and she was gripped by a sudden urgent need to, well, defecate. Black dots did a dipsy-doodle before her eyes.

She caught her balance and stared at the bumper stickers on the SUV behind the motel between where she stood and her own temporary home a motel over. God Hates Fags, and all the rest. And yes, there was that poor lynched doll.

Alice made her feet take a step toward her motel. *Run!* screamed her mind, *Run to your motel!* But no, the feet could only manage that one indecisive step. Her eyes clicked to the right, where the trailers stared back at her. A single security light had come on somewhere behind the first row to fight the darkness; blobs of darkness squatted beneath each trailer, the pink insulation gray in the shadows like Spanish moss in an antebellum horror flick.

Each set of trailer windows reflected lights from the motel, giving them a jolly lunatic leer. *Run away, Alice*, they said. *Or stay, why not?*

Alice looked again at the motel where the SUV was parked. "Call the police," whispered her mind. Her hand reached for her phone, and she held it indecisively in her pocket. What could she say? "I'm being stalked"? Well, that seemed to be true. But how could she prove that if the man denied it, claimed coincidence in travel plans?

She turned again toward her own motel with its arrays of silent watchers behind it and willed her feet to take another step.

Too late! Bushes rustled behind her. Fast footsteps tocked on empty pavement as Alice spun to face the medical building. He was upon her, a hand clamped over her mouth. Her purse slipped halfway down her shoulder. With difficulty she held onto it.

"Lenore, you bitch!" he hissed into her ear. His breath smelled like an old ashtray. "Did you think I didn't recognize you?"

Lenore? Poe's lost Lenore? Was this a literary mugging? Alice's head was clamped between her assailant's hands so she couldn't look around. She rolled her eyes until they strained in their sockets, but she saw nobody else, and no Lenore answered the man.

Up close, this man was amazingly rancid. The obvious tobacco habit had dulled his olfactory nerves to the point where he couldn't tell how much he needed a shower, much less how nasty it was to overlay that smell with cheap aftershave.

"You're coming with me," he announced and began to quick-march Alice along the road toward (oh, no!) the trailer field. He had timed his attack well. Nobody, of course, travelled the access road just now. And she knew that once travelers settled into their rooms and it was dark, they never bothered to look out their windows. Who would want to look at those trailers or an empty access road?

She tried to jerk away, tried to bite, and he gave her head a hard shake, wrenching her neck. "Quit it, Lenore!" The nearest trailer loomed, and then she was swallowed up among their shadows. The deep grass crunched underfoot.

She felt the pepper spray bottle tick uselessly against the inside of her elbow, the one the man clutched in a death grip. Could she reach it, uncap it, hold it the right way before she pressed the trigger? Not really.

He selected a trailer two rows in and stopped. "I'm going to let go for a second. Don't you dare move, or so help me, Lenore, I'll snap your neck like a chicken bone. And you know I can." She had no doubt of that. From a distance he'd looked scrawny and malnourished but close up his arm muscles bulged under the sweaty t-shirt he wore. Its cartoon front showed a grimacing child urinating on a car company's logo.

He took his hand from her mouth. Saliva smeared her chin. She thought it was saliva and not blood, but he'd clamped her mouth so hard that her lip felt torn, so she wasn't sure. She swallowed, tasting salt, and her abdomen clenched; she forced herself not to vomit.

"Who—who's Lenore?" she squeaked.

The man backhanded her, hard. She fell against the side of the trailer. It was true what the novels said. If someone hit you hard enough you saw stars.

"Don't fuck with me, bitch. Do you know how long it took me to find you again? Huh? Who helped you? It wasn't that old bag you've been driving around. Are you in some kinda witness protection plan? That why your hair's different? Who bought that car for you? Some dude you've been messing with?"

"I'm not Len...." Alice saw him raise his hand again; she yelped and wrapped her arms around her head. The purse, unnoticed, slid to the ground.

"Get in there. I'm going to teach you..." He opened the door and grabbed her by the arm. Darkness spilled out of the trailer door, or so it seemed to Alice. The door became a mouth. *Come in, Alice*, it taunted. *Come in and stay, for always.* The trailers on all sides loomed. *Join us, Alice. Be assimilated.*

"Help!" yelled Alice, and then, remembering some advice she'd read somewhere, she changed it to "Fire!"

As she drew breath to shout again, he slammed her head against the trailer door jamb. More stars, and she barely felt herself being lifted bodily, up the stairs. But then he threw her, like a rag doll, inside the trailer. *That*, she felt. Something popped inside her wrist, and she screamed. It occurred to her in her terror what a charmed life she'd led up to now. Nobody, *nobody*, had ever deliberately hurt her before today.

The door admitted a dim slice of light. The man appeared large in the doorway, silhouetted. Alice saw, briefly that his bald freckled head was graced with a few fine wisps of hair that gleamed against the pale light behind him. On a kind man such as her father had been, it would have been sort of endearing. On this one, it added another element of ghastliness.

"Don't you dare try to scream again, Lenore," he said low as he stepped forward. "I can make it *so* much worse for you."

Umber light filtered in through the one grubby window at the end of this narrow room. Looking around wildly, Alice's glance roamed across what looked like construction debris, candy wrappers, and oddments of junk, and found a dark doorway. No way out that way, she realized. It must go to another windowed room.

I'm in the right eye socket of a singlewide, she thought, and choked back a sob that was part giggle.

"You think this is funny? Huh?" His hands were on her, one at her throat, the other wrenching her head back by her hair. She yelped. He released her hair and began to dig in a pocket.

"The guys asked me, 'where's that wife of yours?'" he was saying as his shoulder hitched, one hand in his pocket. Triumphantly, he pulled out a tangle of elastic cords, the kind with hooks at the ends, used for strapping loads onto vehicles. He released her throat and the other shoulder hitched; he dug into the other pocket, which yielded up a bandana and, no. Yes. A knife, its blade protected by a scabbard of cardboard. Her eyes widened further.

"You thought I'd brought my gun, didn't you?" (This sounded like 'dinchoo'). "Naw, too easy for you, Lenore. They laughed! The guys, they laughed at me. Because of you, you dirty bitch, they knew you'd gone off and left me."

He set down the knife and began to organize the bandana.

Alice grimaced in distaste. The bandana looked less than clean, and it appeared she was going to die with it over, or in, her mouth. The word "Gag" was apt, it appeared.

"Wait! At least tell me your name so I'll know who's killing me."

He backhanded her again. "Shut *up*, you stupid bitch!"

"I'm not Lenore!" she wailed, ducking as he aimed another blow, which landed on her ear. It rang, or maybe whistled.

He reached for her head and grabbed it by the hair. This seemed to be his handle of choice. "But now, I gotcha!" He gave her hair a yank for emphasis. The fine hairs at the back of her neck were especially painful. As Alice opened her mouth to cry out, or maybe plead, he shoved the bandana in and tied the ends behind her head, entangling some loose strands of hair and giving them another especially painful pull.

He shoved her back against the wall and picked up the elastic cords. The knife was on the floor somewhere close by. Heroines in novels, Alice knew, would use this opportunity to snatch up the knife and plunge it between his ribs. (Or, in the Koontz/King variety of novel, into his left eyeball, and "matter" would squirt in a particularly mucous-filled metaphor. In some cases, it would go into her mouth but she would ignore it.) She simply didn't have it in her to try this. She stared past his meaty shoulder. Play for time, yes, that's what she should do.

Tears leaked down her face, soaking the edges of the bandana—she didn't know if they were from pain or fear. Oddly, on one level they included pity. Pity for this poor Lenore whose unfortunate resemblance to Alice had gotten her into this disaster. She hoped that at least Lenore would stay hidden from this nameless (Billy-Bob? Bobby-Lee? Johnny-Gee? Surely not just Bubba) thug and would avoid this particular north-south corridor where he had apparently been trolling for his Lost Lenore.

Maybe Lenore was living happily ever after in some small New England town, keeping company with a riotous gang of church ladies. Alice hoped so.

She shook her head. He'd been trying to jerk her hands behind her to wrap the cord around them. This pressed her face into his chest; the smell of him made her gag anew, and her hands *would not* stay still.

"Quit it, Lenore!" He shoved her to the side and leaned behind her, giving her sprained/broken wrist a good hard tug. She wailed; with the gag, the sound came out "Gaaaoooww!"

Odd how the mind plays with terror, she thought again. That trailer door, which had fallen shut behind Billy-Bob but not latched, appeared to be drifting open in the gloaming.

This time, of course, it was her mind's hoping for it rather than her mind's fearing it—how bad could any new monster be, outside that door?

"Got it!" said Johnny-Gee with satisfaction as the hooks snapped together. He sat back on his heels and felt for the knife on the floor.

"Charles told me he seen you out on route 40, in a car with some old lady. She your cover?"

Alice shook her head until her short hair flopped wildly. Not Mom! This horrible man mustn't go after her mother! Bad enough for Mom to have her only daughter disappear without a trace. Alice struggled frantically at the thought and the man smacked her again. More stars. He jerked her back upright.

The door drifted further open silently; Alice stared, mesmerized over her captor's shoulder. A head, crowned with wild curls like a halo in the back lighting. A woman's head, Alice was sure. Oh no, Bobby-Lee has an accomplice? A new girlfriend to heal the ache in his heart after Lenore?

Alice found herself inexplicably angry on Lenore's behalf. Sufficiently awful that he was an abusive murdering sonofabitch, but he was an unfaithful one as well.

The woman glided in. Not the sort of woman Alice would have expected this sort of man to take up with. No high heels on this one. The absolute silence indicated sneakers or bare feet. This woman moved from the shoulders, like an athlete or maybe some large feline thing, strong, sure of herself.

148

Alice shrieked through her gag. The man had begun work with his knife; not a sudden stab to the heart or slash to the throat, but a controlled surgical slice across Alice's cheekbone. A split-second of numbness, then a searing acid burn as air entered the wound. Now Alice hardly noticed the mysterious woman who floated cautiously about behind the man, seeking something in the near-dark.

Billy-Bob wrenched her head to the side, presumably to line up a matching cut on the other cheek. "Hold still, you dumb cunt!" he ordered.

Alice's eyes rolled in terror and saw, behind her torturer, the woman rearing back to swing a clublike object. She looked like a rookie trying out for the major leagues.

"Look out!" Alice tried to shout, though she realized instantly how mad that was.

She tried to duck as the club (it was a length of 2X4, she learned later) swung down and struck with a mighty crack. The force of it sent Bobby-Lee flying. Blood trickled from a small nick beneath Alice's right eye—the knife had gone spinning off into the dark but not without leaving one final mark of its passing.

Alice found herself staring up at the woman who stood, panting and leaning on her chunk of wood, its end darkened. The woman knelt carefully, ignoring the crumpled man next to her and reached for Alice, who flinched back.

"Easy, Lenore," reassured the woman, as to a skittish horse, "Just going to untie you."

She found and unhooked the cords. Alice pulled her hands loose, wincing as her wrist spoke loudly again. Ignoring it as best she could, she pulled the gag from her mouth. More hairs pulled loose; she ignored that as well.

"Thank you," whispered Alice weakly. She rose, took a sideways step, narrowly missing the crumpled body on the floor, and recovered her balance. She wobbled to the trailer door. The unknown woman reached forward to steady Alice as she descended the steps.

"Excuse me," murmured Alice and then spat on the ground to remove the taste of the gag. She retched, and then spat again.

"Careful," warned the woman, "Your purse is around here somewhere. That's how I knew which trailer the screams came from."

Alice used her eyes now and located the purse, happily still dry, some feet away. A siren warbled a block or two distant, growing louder as it neared.

"I called 911 when I heard you yell 'Fire.' Hope I don't get in trouble for clocking your husband."

Alice recoiled. "He's...." she coughed dryly and tried again to speak, "He's not my husband!"

"Boyfriend?"

"Certainly not! I don't even know his name!"

Spotlights picked them out and two uniformed silhouettes strode forward.

"Hands where we can see them, please," a low strong voice called to them. Alice shivered; were all the women in this area possessed of such casual confidence?

"I'm the one who called you," answered her rescuer, "I'm Nan Eldridge. This is Lenore, who was being attacked. Her boyfriend is in that trailer—I think he'll still be unconscious. I hit him with a two-by-four."

"Stop calling me that!" shouted Alice, startling them all. "I'm not Lenore and I never saw that man up close until today!" She covered her face with her hands, then jerked them away. She looked at the blood on them and cried.

*

NAN STAYED WITH HER DURING the police interviews and the long hours in the emergency room awaiting the technician who would insert ten stitches into Alice's face. They rode back to the motel in the rear of the same police car, and now Alice couldn't find her room key.

"Check your wallet?" suggested Nan as Alice hamster-pawed through her purse, "Maybe you tucked it in with your credit cards."

Tears neared the surface again. Alice was exhausted, and she was hyper-sensitively aware of the nape of the police officer's neck, radiating patience to the extreme. She was A Victim, and she felt like it.

"I'm sorry," she said again, and the officer turned and smiled at her.

"No problem. Just ask the night clerk for a spare. Do you need me to go in with you?" The kindness in the woman's smile triggered a quiver in Alice's lower lip. She tightened it (why do they say stiff *upper* lip? she wondered) and gathered her dignity about herself.

"No, thank you. I'll be fine," said Alice.

"I'll go in and get her settled," Nan volunteered.

"I think I should stay with you," Nan announced as Alice argued with her room's access card reader. Alice hated these things. She always put them into the slot facing the wrong way, or left them in the slot too long, or not long enough. She generally managed to open a hotel door after three attempts. "I'm not stupid," she'd think, "but I feel like I am."

Nan continued, "I can just sleep in the other bed—oh." The door fell open, revealing the single king-size bed. "Or I can nap on the chair."

"You don't need to. It's okay". Ignoring this, Nan followed her in.

Alice sagged onto the bed, dropping her purse onto the floor beside her. She knew she needed to shower and brush her teeth but lacked the energy for that first step toward the bathroom. She fell back onto the cover.

Nan busied herself with the in-room coffee maker, leaving Alice to lie on the bed.

"Decaf? Or regular?" she asked and tore open the green packet and placed it into the receptacle. She went to the bathroom for water. She pushed the little red toggle; the machine vomited decaf into the foam cup.

"Tired, so tired," Alice thought. Everything hurt, even her hair. Oh, of course, he had dragged her around by her hair.

This thought galvanized her, and she stood up. She took a step toward the bathroom and staggered, leaning on the back of a chair.

"What gives?" Nan was at her side to steady her.

"His smell! It's all over me. I need a shower, *now*."

"Sit down! You're in no shape to stand up in a slippery tub." She shushed Alice's protests. "I'll draw you a bath."

"Couldn't possibly!" snapped Alice. "Hotel bathtubs, ick!"

"I'll give it a good rinse with hot water," said Nan. "It's either that or I'll have to get in the shower with you to make sure you don't fall down."

"No!"

"Okay then, I'll run you a bath. You sit here and drink this." Nan handed her a cup of hyper-sweet motel coffee and Alice absent-mindedly sipped the nasty stuff. For the first time all evening, Alice felt warm and secure.

*

NOBODY NOTICED NEXT MORNING WHEN Nan accompanied Alice to the motel's "Free, hot breakfast!" where they had coffee (surprisingly good) and waffles (unsurprisingly mediocre).

"Seriously, though," said Nan, continuing the discussion they'd started in the room, "Don't you think you should see a counselor when you get home? Officer Pearson's been trained in this stuff, and she thinks you should. You don't want to have your life ruined by this post-traumatic whatsis."

"Stress syndrome," finished Alice for her. "Isn't that just for soldiers?"

"No, it's anyone who's been through what you have! Alice, you didn't get to sleep until two a.m. and you were exhausted and you still woke up three times. That last time you flailed so much you nearly fell out of bed!"

"Terrible dream! A whole crowd of people were grabbing at me, and they kept calling me by different names. I should be better once I'm home and back to my routine, shouldn't I?"

It seemed to her that the vampires in her favorite novels no longer seemed quite as terrifying. On the other hand, everyone she passed on the street was likely to make her nervous. Only for a while, she told herself, and then she'd get over it.

"I'm not so sure, Alice. What can it hurt to see someone and talk things out?"

"My mother would be horrified," confessed Alice, "She doesn't believe in 'headshrinkers' as she calls them, except for really crazy people."

"Alice, jeez! You're how old, did you say? Forty-four? It's what *you* think! You're a big girl!"

"I don't feel like it," muttered Alice.

"What?"

"I don't feel like a 'big girl'! I did before last night, but now I feel like an incompetent baby! I just went along with that, that...." she shuddered, "That *creep*. I didn't put up a fight; I didn't even try to run away! *You* had to rescue me, a total stranger, and then the police, and that man'll still think I'm his stupid Lenore, why not? So, when he gets out, and you know he will..." she wiped away a tear and winced.

"It's too bad you live alone," mused Nan.

"Mom's been after me to move in with her," sighed Alice, "I've resisted, of course. I'm not that neurotic!"

"I didn't mean your mom, silly. I meant a friend, or even a roommate, even if you have to find someone in an ad. Someone to, you know, just be around the house at least part time. Ask around where you work, or your book club or something."

Alice slumped back in her chair. The hard wooden slats dug into her back, picking out another bruise she hadn't known she had. "I don't have a book club. I don't seem to have the knack of making friends easily. I have some work friends and we go out for dinners, but no..." she shrugged.

"Girlfriends?" suggested Nan.

"I told you, I have girlfriends at work."

"I didn't mean that kind of girlfriend." Nan's grin loosened something in Alice, slightly below her waistline. At least there was *one* place that didn't hurt. She sipped her coffee, hoping it hid her blush. How had Nan known?

"No, uh, not now. There was a girl, my college roommate. Elaine, her name was. We lived together for five years. Then she moved out to be with someone else."

"God, I'm sorry. And you've been alone ever since?"

"Well, I do have to look after Mom." Alice wondered why she felt defensive about this. She rambled on, "Mom and I have always been close. She'd think of such neat things to do when I was a little girl. I remember coming home from school the first day of Christmas break-Mom had prepared a formal tea to celebrate. Lace tablecloth, pastries, little sandwiches, the works. Really, all she wanted or expected of me was that I grow up to be...."

"Happy?"

"No!" Alice was honestly surprised by the suggestion, "A civilized person, is what I was going to say. It's such a small thing to ask, really, but often I'm taken aback by how few people want to be."

"You're certainly right there," agreed Nan, quizzically, "Not brave, honest, or happy, but ... civilized? That's, uh, interesting."

Alice's blush was from annoyance this time. "I didn't think that was such a bad thing."

"Oh, not bad at all," Nan hastened to reassure her, "Everyone would want to be around a civilized person, right?"

"Well, not really, it seems. If that person just lives quietly and likes to read and work in the garden and spends a lot of time with her mom, she doesn't seem to be all that appealing to other people."

"Did Elaine tell you why she was leaving?"

"No, just that she was happy with Barbara." Alice hated the pity she saw on Nan's face and hastened to turn the subject around. "Do you have a, um, a special friend?"

"A partner, you mean? A sweetie? A hunka-hunka burning love?"

teased Nan, and then she sobered. "No, I had a partner, but she's gone. Gone forever, dreadful sorry, Clementine."

"Oh, I am sorry. She found herself a Barbara too?"

"Oh, well, it was complicated. Funny, nobody thought we'd be a good match, we were both too butch."

"What's that?"

"Ohmigod, you don't know what butch is? Argh," she cleared her throat. "I guess you'd say it's women who are more boy than girl. You know, one of the partners will be the one who does most of the driving and the heavier work around the house, and would never be caught dead in a dress."

"Oh. And you're like that?" Nan looked at her, an eyebrow cocked. "Oh, of course, you're like that. Sorry. I see now."

"In our case, we both were. And we were just fine with that, because our personalities went together so well. We played on rival teams in the soccer league, and jogged together, and we both like to cook. The butch thing didn't seem to be an issue, or so I thought. Then Sharon came home one day and told me she was going to transition."

"Transmission?" Alice was lost in this bewildering new world.

"*Transition*. She said that she felt that she'd always been a man, and she wanted to start the reassignment process, take hormones and all. I was completely blindsided."

Alice had heard of transsexuals, of course, but never dreamed of coming this close to what seemed an exotic and distant concept.

"Gosh!" She saw the sadness in Nan's face and realized how insensitive her response was. "I'm so sorry. But couldn't you have just stayed with her, and then be able to really get married and all?"

"No, silly. I'm a lesbian, not a straight woman. I loved Sharon, but I just couldn't do it, live with Sheldon and be happy. I hung in there for a while, but it was just too hard. I'd rather be alone."

"Being alone's not so bad, really. Nobody ever tells you what time you have to come in for dinner or takes the last of the ice cream from the freezer."

"Thanks for the encouragement," said Nan wryly.

*

THEY LINGERED IN THE PARKING lot. Reluctantly, Alice reached for her trunk latch.

"Well, listen," said Nan. I only live a couple of hours from you. I drive over there a lot in the summer for the WNBA games. How about I look in on you?"

"Oh, that would be splendid!"

"Splendid?"

"Well yes, splendid. What's wrong with splendid?"

"Nothing, just teasing."

"Anyway, I've gone to a couple of those games. I don't know anything about basketball, but the players are so beautiful."

"I'll explain the finer points. And I'll bet we can find you some new friends at the games." Nan flashed her quick smile as she passed Alice a napkin bearing a phone number.

"Oh! Let me give you mine."

"Already have it, remember? When you gave Officer Pearson your information. And when you have to come back down here to testify, if you like I can come down here with you."

"Oh." Alice's shoulders slumped.

"You'd rather come alone? Sorry, maybe I spoke out of turn."

"I mean, I'd love for us to come together. I just didn't like to remember I have to come back here at all. I want to go home and forget it ever happened."

"Alice, *do* talk to a counselor. It's important. You don't need to tell your mom about it, but *go*."

"But—I've always told Mom everything. Maybe it sounds silly, but I never had anything I couldn't tell her."

"Like about Elaine, you mean?"

"Well, except for that...."

"It could help you in a lot of ways," urged Nan.

"All right I'll do it," said Alice decisively. She slotted her overnight bag neatly into its space in the trunk and brought the lid down. She turned to Nan, hesitated, then quickly touched her arm.

"Thank you. For my life, I think."

"Oh, well...." It was Nan's turn to be embarrassed. Emboldened, Alice leaned over and gave Nan a quick kiss on the cheek.

Then Alice got into her car, closed and locked her door. She looked carefully in all her mirrors, backed out, turned and drove away.

"Have to tell Mom," said Alice to herself. "I *will* tell her. About Elaine and everything. She'll just have to... deal with it."

But as she drove, Alice couldn't keep from wondering where Lenore was. Was she still alive? And what about Billy-Bob, whose name was actually Justin? Would he be locked up for a good long time? Or was he out already, looking for his lost Lenore?

There is probably more than one strip of motels along America's interstates, where the low-rent havens for travelers hunker amid dubious company: abandoned trailers, deserted malls, gothic castles where vampires lurk....

ACKNOWLEDGEMENTS

My thanks to Steve Berman of Lethe Press, for giving "Geezer Dyke" a look-see and deciding to adopt all the stories into the Lethe family.

And to all my pals in the Village who've cheered my literary progress through the years, and generously shared their foibles and idiosyncrasies with me to knit into the characters in my stories.

And, to my sweetie Harriet, who admires and encourages my efforts and can pounce on a typo like the proverbial duck on a June bug.

ABOUT THE AUTHOR

BECKY THACKER was born 70-plus years ago in Michigan's Upper Peninsula but grew up on military bases around the world. She's been writing since elementary school, and holds an Associate Degree in Computer Processing and a Bachelors Degree in Sociology.

She now lives with her wife Harriet in Indianapolis with seasonal forays into Lillian, Alabama.

PUBLICATIONS:

Five Dollars and An Axe (lulu.com; 2019)

Faithful Unto Death (University of Michigan Press, 2011)

The Amazon Girls Handbook (Wicker Park Press, 2002).

The Chorus Kids' Memorial Day Parade (Seeds and Toads Press, 2006)

"Geezer Dyke" appeared in print in *Drag Noir* (Fox Spirit Press, UK, 2014)

Essays have been printed in *Lesbian Ex-Lovers* (Harrington Park Press, 2004, published simultaneously as *Journal of Lesbian Studies*, Vol 8 #3-4, 2004), *Hear Our Voices* (DVN of Greater Indianapolis, 2002), and *Lesbian & Gay Book of Love and Marriage* (Broadway Books, NY, 1998 Lambda Award Winner).

To contact the author: bthacker.thacker@gmail.com